I0823573

PECOS LAW

Also by Bradford Scott and available from Center Point Large Print:

Border War
Ranger Daring
Doom Trail
Border Blood
Guns of Bang Town
Trail of Blood and Bones
Rimrock Raiders
Bullets for a Ranger
Bullets Over the Border
Hot Lead
Hot Lead and Cold Nerve

PECOS LAW

A Walt Slade Western

Bradford Scott

CENTER POINT LARGE PRINT
THORNDIKE, MAINE

This Center Point Large Print edition
is published in the year 2024 by arrangement with
Golden West Inc.

Originally published in the US by Pyramid Books.

The text of this Large Print edition is unabridged.
In other aspects, this book may vary
from the original edition.
Printed in the United States of America
on permanent paper sourced using
environmentally responsible foresting methods.
Set in 16-point Times New Roman type.

ISBN: 979-8-89164-368-0

The Library of Congress has cataloged this record
under Library of Congress Control Number: 2024943159

1

"I 'pecosed' him" was a sinister and conclusive statement in southwest Texas. To translate, the body was shoved into the Pecos River to reach eventually, via the Rio Grande, the blue waters of the Gulf of Mexico.

There were other ominous things said about the Pecos River:

"Only Judge Colt holds court west of the Pecos."

"The deadline for sheriffs."

A grim warning from the outlaw fraternity to law enforcement officers to stay east of the Pecos' yellow flood.

But the Texas Rangers knew no deadline, Pecos or otherwisc.

Of such things was Ranger Walt Slade, named by the Mexican *peones* of the Rio Grande River villages, *El Halcon*—The Hawk. He sat Shadow, his tall black horse, and gazed at the turgid waters storming deep down between the gray and yellow stratification of the towering narrow ramparts, broken here and there by shallow caves and irregular, perpendicular cliffs that were the rocky walls of Pecos River Canyon.

The vista held a fascination for the trained geologist that Walt Slade was. The river had cut a path through the gray and white rock to varying depths of several hundred feet. The walls of the canyon had cake-like strata; in places sun and seepage had bleached or darkened the surface of the rock, making splayed marks, so that the canyon walls resembled frayed, faded curtains. Much the same as the lesser Devil's River Canyon, a wild land to the west of the turbulent waters, where not so very long in the past the Apaches marauded. And even now it was the habitat of reckless men who flaunted law and order.

But even to this desolate region, progress was coming. An iron bridge spanned the canyon and the river, saving the traveler a long and tedious detour.

Slade crossed the bridge and continued westward through a maze of barren hills. Far to the west were mountains. Those to the left were the far-flung ramparts of the Big Bend wilderness and wastelands. Directly ahead were the first of the ranges that form the mountain barrier of the trans-Pecos area.

All day Slade rode through the bright Texas sunshine. He paused for a bite to eat and a helpin' of oats for Shadow at the little roadside community of Langtry, that basked in the glory of a borrowed name.

Originally it had been known as Vingaroon, probably from the plentitude of wind spiders in the neighborhood, but Judge Roy "Law West of the Pecos" Bean, changed the name to Langtry, in honor of the famous actress Lily Langtry whom, tradition says, he induced to visit his barroom-courtroom there.

Judge Bean was a fair simulacrum of the mythical "Judge Colt," for he held court with a law book in one hand and a Colt Forty-five in the other. Judge Bean's courtroom was, as a rule, quite orderly.

After eating, Slade continued on his way until sunset flamed its glory in the west, through a rough and barren terrain. He drew rein and for a period sat gazing at the chromatic splendor, until the vivid hues began to fade; he was a striking picture atop his great black horse. Very tall, more than six feet, the breadth of his shoulders and the depth of his chest matched his height. A rather wide mouth, grin-quirked at the corners, relieved somewhat the tinge of fierceness evinced by the prominent hawk nose above and the powerful jaw and chin beneath. His pushed-back "J.B." revealed a broad forehead surmounted by thick crisp hair as black as Shadow's glossy midnight coat. The sternly handsome countenance was dominated by long, black-lashed eyes of very light gray. Cold, reckless eyes, but with little devils of laughter lurking in their clear depths. Devils that could leap to the front, if occasion warranted, and be anything but laughing.

The homely, efficient garb of the rangeland—bibless overalls, soft blue shirt with vivid neckerchief looped at his sinewy throat, half-boots of softly tanned leather—acquired grace and dignity from the man who wore it.

Around his lean waist were double cartridge belts, from the carefully worked and oiled cut-out holsters of which protruded the plain black butts of heavy guns.

And from the butts of those big Colts his slender, powerful hands seemed never far away.

Such was Ranger Walt Slade as he sat his horse and gazed at the splendor of the sunset.

"Feller," he said to the cayuse, "unless I dis-remember, and I don't think I do, less than a quarter of a mile farther on is a spring, the over-flow of which forms a pool alongside the trail for a ways. Back in the brush a few yards, where the spring bubbles up, is a little clearing where grass grows and the ground isn't any harder than elsewhere. If we keep on going, we could make it to Sanderson some time tonight, but I don't see any sense in you wearing your legs down to stumps. So I guess we can take another night under the stars and get a fresh start in the morning. Okay?"

Shadow's snort signified it was, so they ambled on.

Slade's estimate of the distance to be covered was good and shortly they reached the spot where the tiny stream trickled from the growth. Shadow pushed his way through the brush to the clearing, where there was good grass, with the spring for water. Slade stripped off the rig and left the horse to his own devices, which were a drink from the spring and a cropping of grass. Now the sun had set and it was getting dark under the branches of the chaparral walling the small clearing on all sides.

Choosing a spot close to the trail edge of the clearing, Slade spread his blanket, sat down and rolled a cigarette with the slim fingers of his left hand. He smoked leisurely, listening to the sleepy chirping of birds in the thickets, then rolled up in the blanket and with his saddle for a pillow was soon fast asleep.

The night was very still, with only the whisper of the little stream, the occasional weird cry of some night bird, and the yipping of distant coyotes to break the great hush. Shadow, his belly lined, had lain down and was apparently as sound asleep as his master.

Overhead, the stars wheeled westward, a low moon glowed. The forces of nature seemed gathering for the coming day.

It was about an hour till dawn when Slade abruptly snapped wide awake and lay listening, without movement, as was his habit when suddenly aroused.

Shadow was blowing softly through his nose,

which was enough to awaken El Halcon, knowing that the horse had heard something that his own amazingly keen hearing had not yet caught.

Another moment and he did catch it; the low pattern, drawing nearer, of hoofbeats on the trail. He quickly estimated the number of cayuses to be five.

Louder grew the rhythmic beat. It slowed, slowed still more, ceased directly opposite from where Slade lay. He could hear the horses sucking water from the pool beside the trail, also the low mutter of rough voices.

To the average ears it would have been but a mutter, but El Halcon could clearly understand the words.

"As soon as the fire gets going good, we go in," said a voice. "We won't have much time, but enough I figure, so long as nobody makes some fool slip. You know just what you have to do, and I don't want any slips, understand? We've been doing all right, so let's continue to do all right."

Slade noted that the particular voice was not rough, but clear, and rather musical. The growled "Okays" were quite different.

A couple more minutes and the jingle of bit irons told that the horses had finished chinking and were shaking the drops from their whiskers.

"All right, let's go," said the clear voice. The beat of hoofs resumed, fading westward.

Slade sat up and began rolling a cigarette.

"Sounded sort of strange," Slade continued. "As if somebody intended to burn something. What, I wonder? Yes, it sounded strange, and somewhat ominous. And I have a hunch it would be a good idea for us to find out. Horse, we are supposed to be on vacation, but I have another hunch, a hunch we are going to get mixed up in something. Yes, I wager that before the sun passes the zenith we'll find ourselves right up to our necks in the soup. Oh, well, no rest for the weary."

Pinching out his cigarette, he rolled his blanket and cinched up. On the trail, Shadow stepped out briskly, and Slade didn't curb him, yet. The mysterious night riders had a start, but Shadow would soon close the distance, as much as his master desired it closed. He would do so even were the horses in front going at racing speed, which they were not—at least they were not when they drew away from the clearing.

It was logical to presume that whatever was in the wind had to do with Sanderson, there being no other town this side of Marathon, more than fifty miles to the west.

In the east the sky flushed scarlet and gold. Spears of light flashed to the zenith, fell earthward. The sun arose in glory, and it was day. Slade quickened Shadow's pace a little, his eyes constantly probing the distances ahead.

He reached down and made sure his heavy

Winchester was smooth in the saddle boot snugged under his left thigh. It was a "special," that Winchester, acquired for Slade by his close personal friend, James G. "Jaggers" Dunn, the famous General Manager and moving force of the great C. & P. Railroad system. Jaggers Dunn got whatever he went after, whether it was a gun or a corporation, and the rifle had been made in accordance with Slade's specifications. It was like to Jaggers himself in that, with El Halcon's eyes back of the sights, *it* got whatever it went after, even if the whatever in question was more than six hundred yards distant; a fully dependable arm that had seen much service.

The trail climbed a long and high rise, and from its crest Slade sighted his quarry just topping another rise quite some distance ahead.

They did not look back, but just the same he pulled his horse into the shadow of the encroaching growth, and his eyes never left the five riders until they had vanished down the opposite sag.

And when, later, he crested that rise, he was very much on the alert. In this section it paid to be at all times, especially where strange riders were concerned. Here more than one man had been murdered for his horse and what he had in his pockets.

The sun was well up the eastern slant of the sky, and Sanderson was no great distance away. The trail climbed slowly to the level of a high plateau, across which it passed in a straight line, rounded a little knoll and skirted the brink of Sanderson Canyon. Then another downward dropping sag to the town that sat in a deep canyon, one wall of which overhung to the main street.

And Sanderson was still a wild frontier town, always had been and doubtless always would be. Outlaws roamed the mountains and canyons of the Big Bend country to the southwest, and trafficked in "wet" herds stolen in Mexico and driven across the Rio Grande. To even up matters, Texas herds were stolen and driven south to where ready buyers waited.

The outlaws came to Sanderson to spend their ill-gotten gains, because of which they were tolerated to an extent, just so long as they let the town alone.

Of late, however, they had begun extending their operations to include Sanderson.

Things were bad enough before the railroad came. After it did put in an appearance, gentlemen, hold onto your hats! It brought more citizens, some of which Sanderson could have done without, more saloons and more trouble. Sanderson became a repair-and-crew-change on the S. P., with large railroad shops and sprawling yards.

There was always plenty of money in Sanderson. In the bank, in the office safe of the railroad station if a pick-up hadn't been made for several days. And the saloons were usually loaded. All of which was a temptation to gentlemen of easy conscience.

Slade rode swiftly across the plateau, for now, because of his cautious approach to the various crests, the mysterious night riders were quite a way ahead of him. And he was experiencing an uneasy presentiment that some deviltry was in the making; the fragment of conversation he had overheard had had an ominous sound.

Because of the tall brush that flanked the trail, he would not be able to see into the canyon until he had almost reached the slope that led to the town.

Abruptly, he uttered an exclamation. Rising into the clear air was a column of smoke, coming from the canyon. His voice rang out,

"Trail, Shadow, trail!"

2

Instantly the great black horse lunged forward and in less than a half dozen strides was going at full speed. Slade leaned forward in the saddle, gazing at the sinister column. Somewhere down below a fire was going strong.

Passing a final bristle of growth, he saw the source of the smoke. At the far edge of the town a building—an old one, from all appearances—was burning fiercely. And toward the fire, men were running from every direction.

Slade swept the terrain below with his gaze. Instantly he spotted a structure, a rather imposing structure for Sanderson, which he did not recall seeing in the course of former visits to the town. From its position near the mouth of the canyon, he judged it to be a new railroad station.

Flames were shooting through the roof of the old building, and showers of sparks, and burning brands that threatened to fire nearby structures. Already ladders were set up against the walls of the one nearest, and men were mounting the ladder with buckets of water. Sanderson had no regular fire department but the citizens were trained against such emergencies, and the bucket brigade was dousing the roof.

All of which Slade took in at a glance. What in blazes *was* in the making, anyhow?

He didn't have to wait long to find out. Looked like everybody in town was at the fire.

"Trail, feller, trail!" he called to Shadow, who extended himself still a bit more. Now he was halfway down the sag.

Everybody at the fire? Not quite! Around a nearby corner bulged five horsemen. All wore black cloth masks that hid their features to the eyes. They swerved toward the railroad station, jerked to a halt in front of it, started to dismount.

But the low thunder of Shadow's hoofs reached their ears. They hesitated, masked faces turning toward the sound. One jerked off his hat and waved it around his head, the rangeland warning,

"Stay away! 'Tend to your own damn business!"

Slade didn't "stay away." He whipped his Winchester from the boot as the light gleamed on shifted metal. The big rifle boomed even as fire flashed from the ranks of the horsemen.

One of the five spun from his saddle as if struck a mighty blow. Answering bullets stormed past the weaving, shifting Ranger like angry hornets, fanning his face, ripping through the crown of his hat. Again the Winchester flamed, and there were two motionless forms lying in the dust.

A voice shouted a command. The remaining three whirled their horses and sped west. Before Slade could line sights a third time, the bulk of the station hid them from view. He reached the building, swerved Shadow past it and caught a glimpse of the racing trio vanishing around a brush-flanked turn in the trail. To follow them around that bend would be taking a foolish chance; they might well hole up and wait, expecting him to do just that.

From the station door rushed a wild-eyed man, his face paper white.

"Good—good heavens!" he stuttered, staring apprehensively at El Halcon. "What—what's going on?" His glance fell on the two bodies lying across from the station door and he gulped in his throat and shrank back toward the open door.

"Don't know for sure just what was in the wind," Slade replied composedly to his question, "but I doubt those gentlemen there, and the three who left in a hurry, intended to purchase tickets.

"Are you the agent?" he asked before the other could speak. "Don't recall seeing you when I was here before."

"Why, yes, I am, took over here last month," was the reply.

"Much in your office safe?" Slade continued. The agent stared at him a moment, then,

"Why—why, yes, there is." Again he stared, and abruptly understanding flooded him.

"Good Godfrey! It was a hold-up!" he gasped.

"Guess that was the general idea," Slade

agreed. "Didn't quite get that far, it seems."

"Yes, thanks to you," said the agent, mopping his perspiring face. "Say! Does such a thing happen often here?"

"This isn't the first time," Slade said. The agent gulped again and mopped the harder.

Now men, attracted by the shooting, had abandoned the fire and were streaming toward the station. Among the foremost was a grizzled old veteran with a big nickel badge that proclaimed "Sheriff" pinned to his shirt front. He halted as if he had run into a stone wall, his jaw dropped and he blinked and stared.

"Slade!" he exploded. "Where the blankety-blank-blank did *you* come from?"

"Over east," was the laconic answer. "How are you, Tom?"

Sheriff Tom Crane wagged his gray thatch and swore. "Looks like you were inspired, or playing one of your blasted hunches," he exclaimed.

"Inspiration and hunches the devil!" Slade growled disgustedly. "I'm supposed to be on vacation for a few weeks. Was planning to visit old John Webb of the Cross W and—some other folks. Sure didn't expect to get mixed up in a ruckus first thing. Anywhere within your blasted pueblo isn't safe."

Sheriff Crane grinned and chuckled, and fished something from his pocket which he extended to Slade.

"Well, here's your deputy sheriff's shield," he said, "guess you're still sworn in as my special deputy."

"I told you I'm on vacation," Slade repeated.

"A notion you won't be after you've heard all the news," the sheriff said, his voice suddenly grim. "We'll have to talk a little later."

With a glance at his face, Slade accepted the shield and dropped it in his pocket.

"Suppose we take a look at what you bagged," the sheriff suggested.

"What about that fire?" Slade asked, glancing at the building which was spouting flame and smoke in every direction.

"Nothing to it, just an old shack due to be torn down," answered Crane. "The bucket brigade boys are taking care of the other roofs. Picked a heck of a time to cut loose."

"A very convenient time," Slade said dryly. "That is from the outlaw viewpoint." The sheriff shot him a glance.

"What do you mean?" he said.

"That it was set, of course," Slade explained. "To draw everybody away from the station. There are almost always a few loafers handing around a railroad station, which could have complicated matters for the robbers. So they employed the fire as a decoy to center attention away from the station. Worked very nicely, giving them a free hand, or so they thought."

"Uh-huh, because the hellions didn't count on you. So you did play a hunch, eh?"

"In a way, I reckon," Slade admitted. Lowering his voice he repeated the conversation he had heard.

"Understand?" he concluded, adding. "At least they didn't blow down a section of cliff to distract attention, as the Crater Moral bunch did, when they robbed the bank."

"Uh-huh, the bunch you cleaned up one of the times you were here before," said the sheriff. "That was a mighty bad bunch, but some of the hellions working the section of late 'pear even worse. Well, I calc'late they'll find the going sort of rough from now on, with El Halcon to buck."

"Suppose we look the bodies over," Slade changed the subject.

The masks were stripped off, revealing hard-bitten countenances that Slade considered quite average, although the crowd, which was steadily augmented by new arrivals, voiced the opinion they were unusually ornery appearing galoots.

"Remember seeing 'em before?" Crane asked.

If anybody did, they refrained from saying so, or at least did not recall contacting them, which Slade felt was not surprising. New faces were continually appearing in Sanderson and attracted little attention. Perhaps later some bartenders might remember serving them, and possibly with whom they associated. Rather too much to hope for, though, he was forced to admit.

"All right," said the sheriff, "some of you work dodgers pack 'em to my office. Don't touch their horses. I'll send a deputy to pick 'em up."

Ready volunteers at once seized the bodies and carried them off. Slade and the sheriff followed, sped on their way by the fervent gratitude of the station agent.

"He was lucky as hell, if he only realizes it," Crane remarked. "Chances are they'd have finished him off."

"Rather logical to assume so," Slade agreed. "What's the news you said you have for me?"

"Believe you mentioned you intended to visit old John Webb," Crane replied. "Well, you'll find him packing his arm in a sling."

"Yes, how come?" Slade asked.

"Rodc around alone in the late evening like he has a habit of doing and spotted some hellions moving away a bunch of his cows," Crane said. "They waved him around, and not being plumb loco, he pulled up. But just the same they cut down on him. Drilled a hole through his arm and knocked him outa the hull. Hit the ground sorta hard, I gather, and was dazed for a bit. When he came back to himself, they were gone and so were the cows. Guess *he* was lucky, too. Reckon they figured he was done for. Anyhow they didn't throw any more lead at him."

"I see," Slade said quietly. His face remained impassive, but his cold eyes seemed even colder, a look in them that Crane well knew.

"So I reckon your vacation notion isn't panning out too well," the sheriff observed.

"I fear you have the right of it," Slade replied. He was very fond of John Webb. Crane nodded his complete understanding.

"Well, after we lay out those carcasses, suppose we amble over to the Branding Pen for a surrounding," he suggested.

"I haven't eaten since early last evening," said Slade, obliquely accepting the invitation. "Did Doc Beard consider Webb's injury serious?"

"Not too bad," Crane said. "Except the shock was not good for a jigger of his age. Guess John is ten or twelve years older than myself, and I ain't a yearling anymore. Reckon Doc pulled him through all right, though. He's still a mite weak but coming along."

They walked on in silence and reached the office. Shadow, who had paced sedately after them, halted at the rack and resigned himself to patience, or so his expression seemed to say,

"Darn loco two-legs! Always gabbin', gabbin', gabbin'!"

Bert Ester, one of Crane's deputies, was in the office and saw to the laying out of the bodies. Ester, unlike the crowd at the railroad station, was always ready to express his opinions and

’lowed he’d seen both of the hellions hanging around town recently.

Slade was inclined to think him right, for Ester, and Charley Blount, the sheriff’s other regular deputy, didn’t miss much and always had their eyes open for questionable-appearing characters.

“Go catch those devils’ horses and stable ’em,” the sheriff told him. Next stop was a livery stable run by an elderly and very competent Mexican who had a warm greeting for both Slade and his horse, shaking hands diffidently with El Halcon and bowing low. He had formerly been introduced to Shadow, a one-man horse who allowed nobody to put a hand on him without his master’s sanction, and the big black received his ministrations with quiet dignity. Slade knew well that the horse would lack for nothing. He and Crane headed for the Branding Pen, a big saloon and restaurant run by a gentleman known as Hardrock Hogan, who had once been a miner and a prospector, until he made a good strike and invested the proceeds in the Branding Pen, which soon justified his business acumen by becoming more of a gold mine than the ledge Hogan had discovered.

Hogan was big and burly with an underslung jaw, a wide, almost reptilian mouth, a crooked nose, narrowed eyes, and bristling red hair. He lived up to his nickname, being plenty hard did occasion warrant, and a firmly rooted “rock” upon which to lean in time of trouble. Also, he was a squareshooter in every sense of the word and ran his place strictly on the up-and-up. Which included drinks, games, and dance floor girls. Nobody had to fear mistreatment or being taken advantage of in the Branding Pen. And if a gent who behaved himself as a gent should had only a couple of pesos to spend, he was made as welcome as his neighbor with a well-lined poke. Live and let live was Hardrock Hogan's motto, and he lived up to it. Slade liked and respected him.

3

As soon as they entered, Hardrock, his sinister countenance wreathed in smiles, hurried to warmly greet the Ranger. The place was already crowded, though the hour was still early, but Hardrock pointed triumphantly to a small table near the dance floor, from which there was a good view of the door, the windows, and most of the room as reflected in the backbar mirror.

"Feller who was down at the station told me you were in town, Mr. Slade, so I cleared everybody away from that table, which was always your favorite," he chuckled. "Passed the word to the Mexican boys in the kitchen, too, and right away they began doing their damndest for El Halcon. Don't bother to order, just tie onto what they'll dish up and you can't go wrong."

Past experience caused Slade to heartily agree.

"Yep, here goes my waistline," said the sheriff. "Eatin' alongside this young hellion is something!"

The story of the thwarted station robbery had been spread around and Slade was the recipient of admiring glances. However, Hardrock shooed everybody away for the time being, so that Slade and the sheriff could enjoy a peaceful meal. For which Slade was duly thankful.

While waiting to be served, Slade elaborated on the incident of the night before.

"It was one of those freakish things that makes you wonder if Something hasn't gotten fed up with hell-raising and decides to take steps to put a stop to it," he said. "If the devils hadn't stopped to water their horses at that pool beside the trail, chances are I wouldn't have roused up for another hour or so, and would have very likely took time to cook a mite of breakfast—still some eggs and bacon in my saddle pouch. So by the time I reached Sanderson, the robbery would have been already pulled.

"But what was said caused me to be a trifle curious and I decided it would be a good notion to trail along after the bunch and try and learn just what they had in mind."

"And played another of your blasted hunches, bless 'em!" said the sheriff.

"In a way, I suppose," Slade conceded.

"And a darn good thing you did, otherwise we'd have been short the money in the station safe, and the station agent," Crane stated with finality.

El Halcon did not argue the point, for he was inclined to concur with the sheriff's diagnosis.

Slade liked the Branding Pen. The bar was long and shining, the back bar pyramided with bottles of every shape and color. The barkeeps could mix any drink desired, but their duties were not onerous where that angle was concerned, straight redeye being the favorite tipple of the Branding Pen habitués.

The dance floor was large, the girls young and pretty. The Mexican orchestra was really good. There were plenty of tables for games, and for those who preferred leisurely dining to grabbing a quick snack at the spotlessly clean lunch corner. Two roulette wheels and a faro bank helped to keep things lively.

All in all, the Branding Pen was a typical frontier town saloon and restaurant of the better sort. And less prone to trouble than most. Hardrock had a couple of floor men about his own size and disposition and a gentle remonstrance on their part was usually enough to stop a ruckus before it really got started.

What interested Ranger Walt Slade most was the fact that, sooner or later, everybody of Sanderson or visiting Sanderson showed up in the Branding Pen.

At the moment, the patrons were the usual varied crowd. Railroaders, cowhands, clerical workers, shopkeepers. Quite a few Mexicans, pleasant, well-dressed, well-behaved young fellows. The majority of them, Slade knew, were employees of the big and lucrative carting train business conducted by John Webb and his niece, Mary Merril. He was acquainted with a number of them, who smiled when they met his eye, and bowed, reverently, to El Halcon.

There were others present not so easy to classify, although as a rule they dressed as cowhands. These last stood alone, for the most part, or in compact groups of three or four, and held little intercourse with their fellow drinkers. They could be just harmless chuck line riders, or they could be something quite different, and *not* harmless. Anyhow they were of the "passing through" variety and quickened Slade's interest.

The meal arrived and was all that had been promised. Slade and the sheriff began doing full justice to it.

"Wonder where those devils came from," the sheriff suddenly remarked.

"Something I've been puzzling over," Slade replied. "I feel pretty sure they had been up to something no good, somewhere. Their horses paced as if they were rather tired, with a good deal of travelling behind them, and the bunch didn't push them."

He paused a moment, then said, "The one who did the talking had a nicely modulated voice, and his choice of words wasn't bad. I would say he was a man of some education and not exactly what one usually runs across in this section.

"But that's the way of it now," he added. "A different type of criminal, different from what we have been accustomed to going up against. More brains, a better understanding of conditions, quick to take advantage of opportunity, and recognizing opportunity. Could be a well-organized bunch, and evidently ruthless. What happened to John Webb bears that out. We may have some serious trouble on our hands."

"Per usual," growled Crane, biting savagely on a hunk of steak. "Never knew it to fail. Hereabouts peace and quiet just ain't."

With which somewhat ungrammatical sizing-up of the situation Slade was inclined to agree.

"Yes, I have a hunch those devils had really been up to something," he said.

Consistently, El Halcon was right; as they would soon learn, this was no exception to the rule.

Just a few minutes later an excited man rushed in, spotted the sheriff and hurried to him, waving a sheet of paper.

"Telegram, Sheriff," he announced. "Just came; agent sent me here with it."

Crane glanced at it, favored El Halcon with a glower.

"Do you ever miss a bet?" he demanded peevishly, and thrust the message at Slade. The Ranger read,

> Store robbed. Think robbers went your way. See you later.
>
> (Signed) Fenwick.

After studying the telegram a moment, his black brows drawing together, Slade returned it to the sheriff.

"As I recall," he said, "Fenwick is manager of the general store at Langtry."

"That's right, manager and part owner," Crane replied. "An old established firm with connections. They do plenty of business. So that's what the hellions had been up to, eh?"

"Logical to presume so," Slade said. "Ambitious gents. Made a haul and were all set to make another. Don't let any grass grow under their feet."

"Uh-huh," growled the sheriff. "But they'll end up with grass growin' over them. Two of 'em already set for it. Here comes Ester. What the devil has *him* worked up? Ain't we going to have a minute's peace!"

The deputy also hurried to the table.

"All right, let's have it," growled Crane. "More trouble, I suppose."

"Not exactly, but sorta interesting," replied the deputy. "I tied onto those two horses and took 'em to the stable as you told me. Went through the saddle pouches and fished out quite a passel of money. I didn't take time to count it, but there's plenty. Left it with Tomas, the stable keeper."

"By gosh!" exclaimed the sheriff. "Part of the Fenwick Store loot, sure as blazes! Wouldn't you think so, Walt?"

"Unless they managed to make another haul someplace, which seems unlikely," Slade answered.

"Well! Well!" chortled the sheriff. "Not bad.

Not bad at all. Gave two of the varmints their comeuppance and recovered some of the loot. Things are working out fine. Now I can really enjoy my surroundings."

"Hate to dampen your ardor," Slade smiled, "but I fear we may have just made a start."

"As the start is, so the finish will be," the sheriff predicted cheerfully, and swallowed a morsel of steak with great relish and gusto.

"And when we get back to the office, we'll go through the pockets of those two horned toads and maybe tie onto some more dinero."

"Not beyond the realm of possibility," Slade conceded. "Sit down, Ester, and have a drink; you've earned it by putting our boss in a good temper."

The deputy laughed, and accepted.

"Mr. Slade, you got both of those devils dead center," he remarked. "Don't you ever miss?"

"The light was good and they were caught sort of off balance," Slade deprecated the feat.

"Just lucky, per usual, eh?" Ester said derisively. "Never before saw anybody who always has everything going his way when it comes to shootin'."

Slade laughed, and let it go at that.

With a sigh of content, the sheriff pushed back his empty plate and nodded to a waiter, who hurried to the bar, knowing exactly what that nod meant.

"That was prime," the sheriff said. "Now a snort coming up to hold it down. How about you, Walt?"

"Another cup of coffee and a cigarette," was Slade's decision.

"Then when you're ready we'll mosey over to the office and give those bodies a more thorough examination. Might just possibly turn up something of interest."

"I didn't touch 'em, and I locked the door when I left," said Ester. "I'll amble back and wait for you fellers."

There being no hurry, Slade sipped his coffee and enjoyed a leisurely smoke. Crane hauled out his pipe and joined him. After which they headed for the office.

"Hellions packin' plenty of dinero on 'em," Crane remarked as they turned out the pockets. "Been doing all right by themselves. Soon as you show up, the county starts gettin' rich. Hello, what's this?"

From a pocket he had drawn two flat circular objects of what looked to be some sort of fiber. To each, on opposite sides, were attached pliable metal strips. Slade turned them over in his hands and his brows drew together slightly.

"Funny things for a jigger with all the appearances of a cowhand to be packing," he remarked.

"What are they?" asked Crane. "Look sorta

familiar—seems I've seen something like 'em before."

"Wouldn't be surprised if you have, if you've fooled around the railroad yards," Slade said. "They are torpedoes."

"Torpedoes?"

"Yes, railroad torpedoes. They fit on top of a rail with the metal strips fitting under the head of the rail and holding them in place. They are small detonating cartridges and when the locomotive passes over them they explode with a sharp crack to warn the engineer to slow down, that there may be an obstruction ahead, such as another train." Crane nodded.

"Wonder what that horned toad was doing with them?"

"Hard to tell," Slade replied, his eyes thoughtful. "Put them in a drawer where there'll be no danger of them being whacked. They're fairly sensitive, and powerful enough to hurt somebody fooling around with them. Well, looks like that's all. Now I'm going over to the Regan House, register for a room, and shave and clean up generally. See you here a little later."

4

After bathing and shaving and donning a clean shirt and overalls, Slade sat by the open window, smoking a cigarette and thinking. Looked like his vacation was over before it began. Oh, well, time and tide waits for no man, as the saying goes, and the same applied to owlhoots with larcenous notions. And he was determined that what happened to John Webb should not go unpunished. Also, according to what Sheriff Crane said, there had been several wanton killings in the section of late, which was of interest to a Texas Ranger.

He chuckled, for he was honest enough with himself to admit that loafing around doing nothing would quickly become boresome. He pinched out the butt of his cigarette and returned to the sheriff's office, where he found Crane puffing on his pipe and contemplating in a complacent manner the blanket-covered bodies on the floor.

"Had the deputies pass the word around to some day-shift bartenders to drop in for a look," he said. "Barkeeps see everything and know everything and maybe one of them will remember something about those two wind spiders. Sit down, I got a pot of coffee bubblin' on the stove in the back room; know you're always in the market for a swig."

"Best thing you've said yet," Slade answered as he sat down.

"Doc Beard says he'll hold an inquest on those two varmints at about eight o'clock, if it's convenient with you," Crane remarked over his shoulder. "Darn nonsense, plant 'em and forget 'em, but guess he figures as coroner he oughta do something to earn his pay."

While they were drinking the coffee, the door opened and a pleasant-looking middle-aged man entered.

"Why, hello, Sam!" exclaimed the sheriff. "You didn't waste any time getting here."

"Wanted to let you know first-hand what happened," the newcomer replied. "Caught the afternoon local. Did you see any of the scoundrels?"

"Got a good look at two of them," the sheriff said cheerfully.

"The devil you did!" said the other.

"Yep," said Crane. "There they are, under those blankets."

The gentleman's eyes widened. "What—what—" he gasped.

"Sit down, Sam, and have a swig with us," the sheriff chuckled. "Walt, this is Sam Fenwick of the Fenwick Store in Langtry. Sam, shake hands with Walt Slade, better known as El Halcon, the owlhoot. He's responsible for getting back a hefty passel of your dinero and doing for those two sidewinders under the blankets. Sit down, Sam."

The thoroughly bewildered store manager mechanically shook hands with Slade and sank into a chair.

"Tom," he pleaded, "will you please stop talking in riddles and tell me what this is all about? You've got me so mixed up I don't know which end I'm standing on."

The sheriff chuckled again and obliged. And the story lost nothing where Slade was concerned.

"Here's the amount recovered," he concluded, handing the manager a slip of paper.

Fenwick stared at it and shook his gray head.

"More than a third of what was taken," he said. "Mr. Slade, I'm greatly beholden to you. And you killed two of them? That's the best of all. It somewhat evens up for our poor devil of a night watchman; they murdered him."

"Yes?" Slade's voice was quiet, but for the second time that day, his cold eyes grew even colder.

"Stuck a knife in his back," replied Fenwick. "He never had a chance. Mr. Slade, I've heard of you—guess everybody in the section has—and the things you did the other times you were here. And I wish to assure you it is not only a pleasure but an honor to meet you in person.

"And," he added diffidently, his face brightened

by a smile, "if you don't mind, I'd like to shake hands again."

Which they proceeded to do, with warmth, while the sheriff chuckled still again and poured coffee.

"Just how was the robbery committed?" Slade asked.

"They drilled out the combination knob and opened the safe," Fenwick replied. "Looked very much like a real professional job, it seemed to me."

"Very likely it was," Slade said. "And the watchman, where was his body found?"

"In the office, close to the safe," Fenwick answered. "He evidently was eating his lunch when he was struck down, for the remains of it were on the table."

"Were the store doors locked?" Slade pursued.

"They were certainly supposed to be," Fenwick said. "I feel safe in saying they were. Poor old Withrow, the watchman, was a very dependable person."

"Old locks, I presume," Slade continued.

"Why, yes," the manager admitted. "It's an old building and I doubt if the locks were ever changed."

"No chore to open such locks with a key made from a wax impression," Slade said. "Or if the key was left in the lock, inside the store, a pair of thin-jawed pliers with which to grip the key and turn it would do the trick. Yes, all the earmarks of a professional job by individuals who knew their business. Now I'd like for you to take a look at those dead men and let me know if you recall seeing them in life."

Crane removed the blankets and the manager studied the dead faces.

"Yes," he said slowly, "I am pretty sure both were in the store more than once recently, making small purchases. They were strangers and we don't get many strangers in Langtry, so I noticed them."

"Getting the lowdown on things," Slade said. "Now one more question, was there an unusual amount of money in your safe last night?"

"Yes, there was," Fenwick replied. "Yesterday we received payment for mining machinery and tools that were freighted north by west."

"I see," Slade said. "So it would appear somebody was able to learn about it. Looks like we're up against something out of the ordinary, Tom, not a stray brand of brush poppers who just happened along."

"Guess you've got the right of it," growled Crane.

Slade abruptly stood up. "You aim to stick around, Mr. Fenwick?" he asked.

"Yes, I think I'll spend the night here," the manager decided.

"I'll take him over to the Branding Pen for a snort or two," Crane put in.

"Okay," Slade said. "See you there later; I'm taking a walk."

Crane contemplated his broad back as he passed out the door, and nodded sagely.

"Going to do a little thinking," he observed to Fenwick. "Says he can always think best out in the open. And what comes of that thinking, certain rapscallions won't like one bit."

"What about that El Halcon nonsense?" the manager asked.

"A sorta funny story," replied Crane. "The Mexican *peones* named him that; means The Hawk. Sorta reminds you of one, don't he? One of the big mountain fellers who'll tackle an eagle and send him hightailing. Walt don't have much to say about himself and he's killed quite a few horned toads with a killing overdue. Which causes some loco hombres to say he's just an owlhoot himself, who takes the law in his own hands and manages to pull the wool over the eyes of some dumb sheriffs. Too darn smart, so far, to get caught, but will get his comeuppance sooner or later.

"Then there are other folks who just know him as El Halcon but stand up for him and tell those other jiggers off proper, pointin' out to 'em that he always works on the side of law and order. Sort of a two-sided reputation he's got."

The sheriff paused to light his pipe and, in deference to Slade's wishes, refrained from mentioning that Slade had acquired that somewhat unusual reputation because of the fact that whenever possible he worked undercover and did not reveal his Ranger connections. Those who knew the truth, including himself, were firmly of the opinion that Walt Slade was not only the most fearless but also the ablest of the illustrious force of law enforcement officers.

"I'll admit it worries me some," Crane resumed. "I'm always scairt some loco marshal or deputy might mistakenly throw down on him. And Walt would be at a disadvantage, not wanting to kill a peace officer. Chances are, though, he'd wing the jigger before he managed to get into action.

"Then, too, there might be some professional gun slinger who'd like to be known as downing the fastest gunhand in the whole Southwest, and ready to shoot in the back. Not that he'd have much luck at slipping up behind Walt, who has ears that hears things before they're said, and eyes like a rabbit, that looks all ways at once.

"Just the same it worries me some, but Walt says that because of what some jiggers think of him, he gets to hear things he otherwise wouldn't, and that hellions who figure him to be just one of their own brand, hornin' in on things, sometimes get a mite careless and later wish they hadn't.

That is if they are lucky enough to be in shape to do any wishing.

"And the *peones* and other poor devils who don't have it so good swear by him, saying he's the good friend to everybody in trouble and in need of help. And they pray to *El Dios* to always watch over him and keep him safe. Walt says that means more to him than anything else."

"He's right," Fenwick said soberly. "Pray earnestly for others and it's likely your prayers will be answered."

"Amen!" said the sheriff.

For some little while, Slade wandered about aimlessly. He walked Railroad Street, contemplating the bustling activity of the yards, pausing from time to time to exchange a word with trainmen he recalled from previous sojourns in the section. He entered several places, including thc Hog Wallow saloon run by a corpulent gentleman named Cruikshanks, who at the moment was asleep in the back room, his usual habitat during the early afternoon and evening hours; he roused up with the owls, sometimes. Slade liked him.

Gradually Slade worked his way toward the mouth of the canyon, to a point from which he would have a good view of the sunset. Rolling and lighting a cigarette, he gazed absently westward, pondering recent occurrences, lounging comfortably against the sturdy trunk of a tall dead tree that lifted naked branches to the sky. He turned his head slightly at the sound of hoofbeats.

Three horsemen were riding out of town at a fast pace. Without appearing to do so, Slade watched their progress. Why all the hurry? He wondered.

As they drew nearer, they abruptly slowed their gait quite a bit. He noted eyes slanting in his direction. They came opposite where he stood, and about thirty yards to the east.

The next instant, Slade was behind the stout tree trunk, both guns blazing. Answering slugs thudded into the tree trunk, chipped off chunks of bark. He shot with both hands, saw one rider lurch forward, recover, stay in the hull. Again he lined sights as best he could around the massive hole of the tree. A wailing curse echoed the reports. Then they were past, going like the wind. Slade angrily emptied his Colts in their direction, but now the range was overly great for sixgun work and they kept going, swerving westward into the trail that ran past the canyon mouth. Another moment and they whisked out of sight around a bend. Slade gazed after them a moment, reloading his guns.

"Well, the devils didn't waste much time trying to even the score," he remarked to the friendly tree trunk. "Mighty glad, feller, you chose this particular spot to grow. You came in mighty handy and stopped quite a bit of lead. Thanks a lot. Now I'll use you to lean against for a while longer, and watch the sunset."

He glanced toward where several men, attracted by the shooting, were converging on him, cautiously, and decided there was nothing off-color about them.

"What's going on, cowboy?" one called.

"Some gents prematurely celebrating Fourth of July, I guess," Slade replied, hoping the spent cartridge shells on the ground would not be noticed, for he was in no mood for explanations.

"Always some loco coots pepperin' holes in the sky," said the speaker. "Mighta hit an angel!"

There was a general laugh and the group turned back the way they had come. Slade concentrated on the glowing beauty of the sunset.

Nevertheless, his thoughts were busy with the recent occurrence. He wondered was it the same three that skalleyhooted west after the abortive attempt to rob the railroad station. Could be, although he recalled that one of the former trio was tall and broad-shouldered, while the three that tried to stage an out-in-the-open drygulching were all middle-sized men. Anyhow, there was little doubt but that they were members of the same bunch. And that it was a bunch that had to be reckoned with. Now he was convinced that it was a well-organized and perhaps numerous outfit. Yes, looked like there were busy times ahead of him.

5

Until the riot of colors faded in the west and the stars burned through the sable vault of the sky, Slade stood leaning against the tree. Then he turned and slowly made his way to the Branding Pen, thinking deeply the while.

When he entered the Branding Pen, he found Crane and Fenwick awaiting him; the former eyed him suspiciously.

"Plumb certain I heard shooting somewhere a while back," he said. "Well, what was it?"

Slade told him. The sheriff said a number of things, none of them complimentary to the three would-be drygulchers. Fenwick regarded the Ranger with wondering admiration.

"How in the world did you guess in time what they had in mind?" he asked.

"They telegraphed their intention when they slowed up and paid me too much attention as they drew near," Slade explained. "So when they reached I was prepared, and that old dead tree was mighty convenient and gave me the advantage. If it hadn't been handy, the story might have had a different ending."

"I doubt it," said the manager. "I've a notion you would have taken care of all three of the scoundrels no matter what the circumstances were."

"No doubt about it," the sheriff seconded heartily.

"Thanks for your confidence, both of you," Slade smiled. "How about a bite to eat? A brush with drygulchers always makes me hungry."

"Had it been me, I wouldn't have had any appetite for a week," Fenwick sighed. "As it is, I believe I can put away a surrounding, as the cowboys say, a small one."

"You'll get a big one, and you'll put it away," predicted Crane. "Just wait and see what the kitchen boys dish up. When this young hellion is here, they sure do their damndest."

When the food arrived, both of the sheriff's predictions were speedily justified.

"And now a couple of snorts," he told the waiter. "That's right, two. This young coot will just be swiggin' some more coffee. He'll end up turning into a coffee bush."

"I prefer a little beautiful redeye," grunted Crane. "How about you, Sam?"

"I'm inclined to string along with you, Tom," Fenwick replied. "Perhaps he'll change as he grows older."

"Not for the better, on that you can bet your last peso," the sheriff declared energetically.

Leaving the two oldsters to continue the discussion alone, Slade went back to the kitchen to thank the cook and his helpers for their thoughtfulness, and left them beaming.

"And now how do you feel?" Crane asked when he returned to the table.

"I feel like just relaxing and taking it easy for a spell," Slade replied. "Enough excitement for one day. Tomorrow I hope to ride to the Cross W and see how John Webb is making out."

"And how Mary Merril is making out, eh?" remarked Crane.

"I wouldn't be surprised if I run into her," Slade smiled.

"A fine young woman," Fenwick interpolated. "I've done some carting business with her. Webb and Arista have just about turned the business over to her. They are wise in doing so; she's sure expanded the operation in the past year. Yes, she's a fine girl. Pretty as a picture, too."

With both statements, Walt Slade was emphatically in agreement.

"What about the inquest?" he asked. "It's already past eight."

"Doc Beard had to visit a patient and put it off till tomorrow, right after noon," the sheriff replied.

The evening wore on, with the Branding Pen growing livelier by the minute. It was a bit past midnight when Slade suddenly exploded,

"Well, I'll be hanged!"

A girl had pushed through the swinging doors. She wasn't very big, but what there was of her left nothing to be desired, figure-wise or otherwise. Her eyes *were* big, astonishingly so, and darkly blue. Her lips were vividly red, her glowing cheeks sun-golden under their bloom. A few freckles powdered the bridge of her straight little nose. Overalls and a soft blue shirt, well open at the throat, enhanced rather than detracted from her proportions. The broad-brimmed "J.B." she hauled off as she entered revealed a mop of dark, curly hair with glints of red in it, that clustered about her piquant little heart-shaped face.

And the sway of her hips as she crossed the room was calculated to totter the equilibrium of an impressionable young man, or of an impressionable older one, for that matter.

Such was Mary Merril, half-owner of the big Cross W ranch, and half-owner of a lucrative carting business.

"Hello, Mr. Fenwick," she said. "Sorry to see you in such bad company. Hello, Uncle Tom. Hello, dear," to Slade, who had risen to greet her. "One of the boys was in town when the trouble occurred at the railroad station and rode to the spread to tell me you were here. Figured I'd better come in before you mavericked off someplace, or was otherwise—occupied."

Slade favored her with an indignant glare that did not seem to impress her much.

"You imp! You'll give me a stroke or something, riding around over the range alone at this time of night!" he told her.

"I wasn't alone," she replied blithely. "Had Rojo, my horse, with me. Aren't you glad to see me?"

"Sit down and stop asking darn fool questions you already know the answer to," he told her severely.

"Yes, dear," she replied meekly and occupied the chair he drew out.

Old Hardrock came plowing across the room, waving a bottle and grinning broadly.

"Your favorite, Miss Mary," he said. "What only you and me drinks. On the house, of course. In the Branding Pen, always on the house for beautiful ladies."

Mary rewarded him for the compliment with a dazzling smile and graciously accepted the brimming glass.

"And now I want to know just what did happen at the station," she said. "Clyde's account was sketchy. You do the talking, Uncle Tom, there's never getting the straight of anything out of him."

The sheriff obliged. "And that ain't the half of it," he concluded. "Sam, tell her what happened at the store."

Fenwick did so. Mary shuddered when the murder of the night watchman was described.

"And now, Walt, I guess we'll have to let you tell her about the drygulching, seeing as you were the only one there."

Mary sighed and shook her curly head when Slade finished his brief account.

"Always trouble," she said. "Seems the section is getting worse instead of better. Well, I suppose I shouldn't complain. At least, it brings him back to me."

"I happen to know this time he was supposed to be on vacation and rode over here for the express purpose of visiting you and Uncle John," said the sheriff.

"That helps," Mary said. "That he planned to spend his vacation with me instead of with another of his women."

"Bet he hasn't got any," Fenwick put in before Slade could frame an appropriate denial.

Mary smiled again, enigmatically, and did not further pursue the subject.

After a while, Fenwick glanced at the clock. "Afraid I'll have to be toddling," he announced. "I'm not used to such late hours."

"It is late, and I'm tired," Mary said. "Come on, Walt, walk me to the hotel."

Both Fenwick and the sheriff chuckled.

The inquest got under way late, around mid-afternoon, due to the coroner putting in a tardy appearance. However, it was brief, the verdict of the coroner's jury 'lowing the two outlaws got exactly what they deserved, and hope was expressed that soon there would be more in a similar condition.

"Now what?" asked Crane, after the court had

cleared out in search of refreshment and the undertaker had removed the bodies.

"Now I'm going to pick up Mary at the Branding Pen and we're riding out to the Cross W," Slade replied. "I'm anxious to learn how old John is making out. I'll be back around noon tomorrow, though, if nothing happens to delay me."

"Chances are something will and you won't get back till after dark," Crane predicted pessimistically. "That's usually the way you manage to do things. Okay, take care of yourself; you had a sample yesterday evening of what those sidewinders are capable of. Don't take chances. Guess you'll be safe with Mary along, though. She's darn good company when the going gets rough."

"Good company at any time," Slade said cheerfully. "Anyhow, I don't figure anything will cut loose; just a peaceful ride, and it's a nice day for a ride."

"Be dark 'fore you get to Webb's casa," said the sheriff. "So watch your step."

Slade promised to do so and headed for the Branding Pen where he found Mary awaiting him. They said goodbye to Hardrock, made their way to the stable and cinched up. They spoke but little as they rode through the golden sunshine, for the beauty of the scene charmed them to silence. The sun was low in the sky when they reached Echo Canyon, the gloomy gorge that was the short-cut to Webb's holding.

"I love this place," Mary said.

"Some terrible things have happened here," he reminded her.

"Yes," she said, "but it was here I first met you, up top the cliffs, when I stood hidden and listened to you singing the beautiful song you had composed, and nearly got myself shot when I stepped out of the bushes and surprised you. And you nearly shook my teeth loose when I reached for Shadow after you told me not to, and he came close to taking my arm off because I hadn't been properly introduced."

"You scared the devil out of me when you did it, that's why I shook you," he said.

"I think," she remarked pensively, "it was then I fell in love with you, when you shook me; it was a new experience."

"Quite a day of new experiences for you, wasn't it?" he said teasingly.

"Never mind that!" she retorted. "Sometimes you talk too darn much. I'm always in a state of tremulous apprehension over what you may cut loose with next, especially if there's company around."

Slade laughed, and glanced at the towering cliffs that overhung the canyon.

"Like to ride up there?" he suggested.

"Oh, let's!" she exclaimed. "I'd love to. We're

in no hurry and it will be nice riding through the moonlight."

When they reached the north mouth of the canyon, Slade turned east and shortly they came to a narrow trail that wound up the heavily brush-grown slope to the cliff top. They turned into it and before long reached the crest, where they had a splendid view of the rangeland, east, west, and north. Now half of the sun was below the horizon and the shadows were lengthening; soon it would be dark under the chaparral. For some minutes they sat their horses, gazing at the peaceful scene, then dismounted and walked to the cliff edge.

"It was right here you were standing," Mary said. "I'll never forget. How quiet and restful it is now. But the beautiful echoes are gone since the rock sounding board back of the cliffs was blown down during that terrible fight you had with Juan Covelo and his outlaws. Remember how they sounded when the wind soughed gently through the canyon, a haunting threnody, like horns of elfland softly blowing."

"Yes," he replied. "That thin wall of rock rising from the cave floor back of the cliffs was like a giant tuning fork that sound waves caused to vibrate and put forth that weird music, meaning, sobbing, rising and falling, an eerie fantasia, as the breeze died down to rise again. Well, it is no more, but the memory lingers on."

Slowly they walked back to where they had left

the horses, and Slade swept the rangeland with his keen gaze. Now the sun had almost set, but the level, reddish rays still clearly outlined all objects.

Abruptly, Slade's gaze centered. A mile or so to the west a horseman was riding eastward at racing speed. And several hundred yards to his rear were six more mounted men, also sifting sand. Both the single rider and the others were hugging the brush at the foot of the slopes.

"What the blazes!" Slade wondered aloud. "Looks like they're chasing that fellow."

Undoubtedly they were, for even as he spoke, smoke puffed from the ranks of the group. The crackle of the distant guns was like to thorns burning briskly under a pot. But they quickly loudened. Slade stared at the drama taking place below.

Now the lone rider was almost opposite where Slade and Mary stood at the lip of the slope, close enough for the eyes of El Halcon to take in the details of form and face.

"Mary!" he exclaimed. "That's Joyce Echols, one of your hands."

He whipped his Winchester from the saddle boot and flung it forward.

Slade sent his first bullet whining in front of the pursuers, a gentle hint to pull up.

They didn't heed the warning. And just as he could see them, they could see him. There was a gleam of lifted metal and a slug whistled past, fairly close.

Again the Winchester jutted forward. And this time El Halcon meant business.

The range was long, the angle bad, but just the same, as the big rifle flamed a second time, a man spun from his saddle to strike the ground and lie motionless. Instantly his companions swerved toward the bristle of growth and out of Slade's range of vision.

"Good heavens! They were trying to kill Joyce!" Mary gasped. "Weren't they?"

"They were," Slade replied grimly. "Quiet and let me listen. I don't like this."

6

The utter stillness at the base of the slope was indeed ominent, for undoubtedly the bunch had halted their horses. And then to Slade's ears came a small sound, as if a stealthy foot had come down on a brittle, leaf-covered branch, some distance down but not at the base of the slope.

Slade shot a glance at Echols, the fleeing cowhand, who was now small in the distance.

"Into the brush," he told Mary. "Leave the horses where they are. The devils are coming up and they don't intend to just say hello."

He led the way into the chaparral a few paces, paused.

"This should do it," he whispered. "Lie down, and stay down. You won't help me by getting up. So hug the ground."

"Yes, dear," she breathed tremulously.

Slade laid the Winchester beside her and glided three more paces to the right. She should be pretty well out of range did lead start flying, and he was quite sure it would.

Tense and ready, hands on the butts of his Colts, he waited, straining his ears to catch the slightest sound.

They did catch it, what any ears other than El Halcon's very likely would not have; the slither of a boot on the dry leaves, close. He drew both Colts and sprayed the vicinity of the sound with lead, and instantly changed position, crouching low.

There was a choking cry, and a thump as of something falling. The growth exploded into a blazing inferno of gunfire. Slade shot again, weaved aside, and shot again.

Back and forth gushed the orange flashes. It was a veritable macabre dance, shadowy phantoms blasting death through the gloom, for now it was nearly dark under the branches.

A scream knifed through the roar of the guns, crescendoed to a bubbling shriek, and cut off shortly. At the same instant, two dimly-seen forms loomed directly in front of Slade. He fired, and one vanished. The other lined sights with the Ranger's breast.

But before he could squeeze trigger, fire spurted from the ground nearby, and the thundering boom of Slade's Winchester. The outlaw spun around like a top and plunged forward onto his face. He did not move again.

And now there was noise aplenty, a tremendous crackling and crashing, fading down the slope. Evidently the two devils still on their feet had had enough and were hightailing as fast as they could.

"Keep down," Slade said in a low voice to Mary, "till I make sure of the three that stayed with us."

For tense moments he stood listening, but only the soft whisper of the prostrate girl's breathing was to be heard.

"Guess everything is under control," he said as he began reloading his guns. "You can get up now. And thanks a lot for saving my worthless hide. That's just what you did."

Mary scrambled to her feet and ran to him, sobbing and moaning, shudders racking her slender form.

"You all right?" he asked anxiously, gathering her close.

"Y-yes," she replied. "I'm fine. It's just that— just that I never killed a man before. But I had to; if I hadn't, he would have killed you."

"He certainly would have," Slade agreed soberly. "Come on, back to the horses, and see if Echols kept on going."

When they reached the crest of the cliff, they saw a single horseman advancing slowly from the east.

"Guess he heard the shooting and saw that pair sifting sand away from here and decided to take a chance at coming back," Slade said.

His great voice rolled down the slope. "Everything under control, Joyce! Come on up."

A jubilant howl responded and Echols spurred ahead. Another moment and they heard his horse clattering up the trail.

"Slade!" he whooped as he bulged from

the growth. "I knew it! When I heard all that shootin', I knew it. Knew darn well the hellions had run into you. I pulled up and turned around pronto. Then I saw two of the devils headed west like scared hounds. But, feller, you sure saved my bacon for me. The sidewinders were gaining on me, fast."

"What was it all about, why were they chasing you?" Slade asked.

"I'm darned if I know for sure," Echols replied. "I was riding along the base of the sag to see if any of our critters had strayed into the brush; they do sometimes. Something made me look over my shoulder and I saw those six devils riding my trail. Somehow they didn't look to me like they were up to any good. Sorta leary of stray bunches after what happened to Mr. Webb. So I speeded up a bit. They speeded up, too. I speeded up some more, and they speeded up some more. So I decided to go home, if I could. Wouldn't have made it if it wasn't for you, though. I figured I was a gone goslin' until I heard your gun shoot up here and saw one of the horned toads hit the ground. Just the same I kept going a little longer until I heard all hell bust loose up here, then I turned back."

"Looks like they had some deviltry in mind, perhaps a little chore of widelooping," Slade said thoughtfully. "And didn't want you left alive as a possible hindrance. Well, let's see what the bag is. There's a stand of soto there beside the chaparral, and the dry stalk make good torches."

The sotol stalks were secured and they entered the growth with the makeshift torches burning.

"Here's the one Mary did for," Slade said as they came on the first body.

The girl shuddered again. "Oh, don't talk about it," she begged. "He looked so awful when he fell."

"He looked darn good to me," Slade differed. "Right then I happened to have a couple of empty guns in my hands, and he was lining sights."

"Here's one that got it through the neck," Echols exclaimed. "And you caught this other one dead center. What we going to do with them?"

"Leave them as they are for the sheriff to see," Slade decided. "Do you recall seeing them before?"

Echols shook his head. "Mean lookin' varmints," he growled.

"About average," Slade said. He gazed at the bodies for a moment, his eyes thoughtful; arrived at a decision.

"Mary," he said, "I'm heading back to town to report this business to Tom Crane. You can go ahead to the casa with Joyce if you wish."

"I'll do nothing of the kind," Mary stated flatly. "I'm riding with you. Joyce, you can tell Uncle

John about what happened and that we expect to see him tomorrow."

"Sure for certain," the cowboy replied cheerfully. "All set to go?"

"I expect we'll find some horses down on the range," Slade said as they descended the slope. "I don't think the ones ridden by these four followed the other two."

When they reached the level ground, Slade's prediction proved correct. All four animals, good-looking beasts, were nosing the grass and offered no objections to their rigs being removed. They could fend for themselves until picked up.

"What about the brands?" Echols asked. "Do they tell you anything?"

"Cleverly altered Arizona or west New Mexico burns, I'd say," Slade replied. "Mean nothing."

The fourth dead man also proved to be a stranger so far as Echols was concerned. Slade deferred judgment on all four until he and the sheriff had a chance to give them a more thorough examination.

Echols, his horse somewhat rested, headed for the Cross W ranchhouse at a good pace.

"Well, not a bad day," Slade remarked as he and Mary entered dark Echo Canyon. "Saved a valuable life and rid the earth of four reptiles it can well do without."

"It was a wonderful decision you made, to ride up to the cliff top," the girl said. "Otherwise poor

Joyce would be dead now. Seems almost as if it was ordained we should do just that."

" 'There's a destiny that shapes our ends,' " Slade quoted soberly.

They rode on, the beat of their horses' hoofs loud in the great stillness. When they reached the south mouth of the canyon, Mary exclaimed.

"Look! There's the moon! I said it would be nice riding in the moonlight, and here we are!"

"But headed in the wrong direction, according to our original plans," Slade said.

"When I'm with you, any direction is the right direction," she returned blithely. "But goodness gracious! What will Uncle Tom have to say?"

"Uncle Tom" had plenty to say when they found him in the Branding Pen with his snort and his pipe.

"Well, one thing is sure for certain," he concluded. "You're thinning 'em out. An even half dozen now."

"Yes," Slade agreed, "but as to who is the head of the outfit—and I'm convinced there *is* one, with plenty of know-how—we haven't the slightest inkling. Not even a suspect. And until we do get a line on him, we can look for more trouble."

"Just a matter of time," the sheriff predicted cheerfully. "You don't figure he was one of that bunch tonight?"

"Not according to the vague description we

have of him," Slade replied. "Certainly not one of the four we managed to down. As to the pair that escaped, of course I can't say for sure, but in my opinion, no. In fact, I gravely doubt he was with the bunch. If he had been, I feel he would not have countenanced that loco attempt to smoke us out on the cliff top. That was the sort of impulsive act to be expected from 'hired hands' who can carry out instructions but are not good at thinking for themselves."

"May learn 'em not to try tricks on El Halcon," said Crane. "Especially when he has his gal along."

"She sure came in handy this time," Slade replied. "Was beginning to look a little as if my number was up, but she knocked it down."

"Remember your saying," Mary admonished, "that if it isn't up, nobody on earth can put it up. I imagine Joyce Echols is thinking something like the same thing about now."

"Whoever heard of a cowhand that could think!" snorted the sheriff.

"Well, Walt was one once," Mary pointed out.

"Uh-huh, but he didn't stay one, which shows he *can* think," retorted the sheriff. "Well, I'll tie onto a wagon in the morning and amble out there and collect the carcasses and pack 'em in. More work for Doc. You'll be going along, of course, Walt?"

"Yes, and then Mary and I will make another

try at reaching the Cross W," Slade answered. "Imagine old John is fit to be hogtied about now."

"Oh, he never worries much when I'm with you," Mary said. "He knows you'll take care of me properly."

"Which should give him cause for real worry," the sheriff commented dryly, and was rewarded for his presumption by the wrinkling of a pert nose.

"Doubt if those horses have strayed far," Slade said. "Good-looking cayuses."

"What they'll bring will pay for planting the hellions," Crane remarked cheerfully. "You didn't go through the pockets?" Slade shook his head.

"I wanted you to see everything just as it was," he explained. "After all, you are the chief law enforcement officer hereabouts."

"Or so folks think," said the sheriff. "I've noticed some look a mite surprised when you give orders and I obey 'em and don't arg'fy."

"I try to frame them in the form of a suggestion," Slade smiled.

"Uh-huh, like a mountain lion does when he charges," said Crane.

"And just wait till they see what I'll pack in," he chuckled. "They'll rare up on their hind legs and howl!"

"Speaking of suggestions," said Mary, "if we aim to get an early start in the morning, suppose we call it a night."

7

When they reached the north mouth of Echo Canyon the following morning, they found the bodies right where they had been left. And once again Deputy Ester was confident he had seen at least two of the outlaws in town at one time or another. Charley Blount, the other deputy, was inclined to agree. But both were vague as to where and under what circumstances.

The pockets of the dead men revealed nothing of importance save a rather small amount of money.

"I've a notion the devils are feeling the need of a little ready cash," Crane observed.

"Which means they will be on the lookout for an opportunity of replenishing their exchequer," Slade said. "Yes, they'll very likely strike somewhere soon. Up to us to endeavor to anticipate what their move will be. If we can, we'll possibly be able to prevent another murder or two; it's a killer band."

The horses the four had ridden were located not far off, by a trickle of water. They were tandemed behind the wagon, the rigs piled in the bed, alongside the bodies.

Crane and the deputies headed for town with their grim cargo. Slade and Mary resumed their much-delayed way to the Cross W ranchhouse.

As they rode north to the short-cut through a narrow range of low hills that led to the casa, they sighted a horseman advancing to meet them. Mary gazed toward him and said,

"Why, it's Mr. Griswold Hale who recently bought the Rocking L to the north of our spread, not long after you were here the last time. Appears to be cooperative and with progressive ideas. Uncle John rather likes him."

"And you?"

Mary shrugged her slim shoulders.

"Don't fish for compliments, Mr. Slade, you know very well where my interest lies."

Slade laughed and eyed the approaching Hale.

"Rather nice-looking, don't you think?" Mary said.

As Hale drew near, Slade was inclined to agree. He was tall, well-formed, with a straight-featured face, a firm mouth, dark hair and dark eyes.

Hale waved a greeting and they drew rein together. Mary performed the introductions.

"A pleasure and an honor, Mr. Slade," Hale said as they shook hands, Hale's grip firm but not pronouncedly so, although Slade sensed there was plenty of power in his big hand. "I've heard of you from several sources."

"Gossip is fleet of feet," Slade replied smilingly.

"I'd not put what I've heard in the category of

gossip," Hale returned in his pleasantly modulated voice. "How about you, Miss Mary, hasn't what you've heard been complimentary?"

"As to whether what is said is complimentary or not depends largely on the source," the girl replied.

"That's enigmatical, but not far from the proven facts," Hale said, smiling. "Well, I'll have to be moving on. Want to learn if some equipment I ordered has arrived. I'm putting down a couple of wells to augment my water supply, which is none too good."

"Artesian?" Slade asked casually. Hale shot him a quick look.

"Why, I hope so," he replied. "I'm not sure, of course, knowing little about such matters, but I'm hoping."

With a nod and another smile he rode on. Slade's eyes slanted sideways after his retreating form.

"Walt, why did you ask him what you did?" Mary said.

"Just curious," Slade replied. "He'll get artesian water, all right, water that spouts into the air from a subterranean reservoir under pressure. The configuration of the hills establishes that, in my opinion. And the fact that he expects artesian wells to come in evinces some knowledge of geological conditions, which is not the case with most cowmen."

Mary asked no more questions, but her expression showed she was still curious as to what might be building up in his mind.

Well, if he was of the opinion that Hale would get artesian water from his drilling operations, Hale would get it. There were no secrets between them and Mary Merril knew the truth about Walt Slade.

Shortly before the death of his father, which occurred after financial reverses that resulted in the loss of the elder Slade's ranch, young Walt had graduated with high honors from a noted college of engineering. He had intended to take a postgraduate course in special subjects, including geology, which had always interested him, to round out his education and better fit him for the profession of engineering, which he had planned to make his lifework.

This, however, for economic reasons became impossible, and Slade was somewhat at loose ends. So he lent a receptive ear when Captain Jim McNelty, the famed Commander of the Border Battalion of the Texas Rangers, with whom Slade had worked some during summer vacations, suggested that he sign up with the Rangers for a while and pursue his studies during spare time.

So Walt Slade became a Texas Ranger. Long since, he had gotten more from private study than he could have hoped for from the postgrad. But, as canny old Captain Jim quite likely expected, he had become absorbed in Ranger work, which offered so many opportunities to right wrongs and help the deserving. He hesitated to sever connections with the illustrious body of law enforcement officers and concluded to stick with the Rangers a while longer, although he had received lucrative offers of employment from such giants of the industrial and financial worlds as oil millionaire and former Texas Governor Jim Hogg, John Warne "Bet a Million" Gates, the Wall Street tycoon, and General Manager James G. "Jaggers" Dunn of the great C. & P. Railroad system. After a while, perhaps. Right now he was a Ranger, and content.

And, being honest with himself, he admitted the lure of dim trails, and the "thing" just beyond the far-flung horizon. To say nothing of the fascination of pitting his wits against ruthless and clever men whose genius somehow had taken the wrong fork in the trail, and who had no respect for law and justice.

As they neared the Cross W ranchhouse, Slade gazed north toward Griswold Hale's holding, which ran back into the northern hills. They were loftier, those hills, than the shallow rises to the south, more rugged, slashed by gorges and canyons. Between the two ranges, the level prairie formed a wide trough. Yes, Hale's drilling would very likely bring in spouting artesian water; the geological conditions were ideal.

Old John Webb, looking a little pale, his arm in a sling, greeted Slade warmly.

"Echols told us about what happened last night," he said. "But he was sorta ramblin'. Suppose you fill in the chinks, Mary."

The big-eyed girl did so, in a manner not at all detrimental to Slade, who at once insisted it was her courage and quick thinking and acting that had saved him from getting his comeuppance.

"So! All set to cut a notch in your gunstock, eh?" Webb chuckled.

"It wasn't my gun, it was Walt's rifle," she protested. "Besides, I'd rather not hear any more about it."

"Once a killer, always a killer, or so they say," her uncle replied cheerfully. "Gets to be a habit with folks. Watch your step, chick, or you'll end up a listening woman."

"A listening woman!"

"That's right," Webb said. "With your head slanted a little to one side, listening for a dead man to whisper over your shoulder. I once knew a feller who always carried his head that way. He *was* the sort that cuts notches, and he'd cut eighteen of 'em, best as I can rec'lect."

"Your sense of humor is reprehensible!" Mary said. "I'm hungry!"

"You always are," replied Uncle John. He winked at Slade. "She'll make some cowpoke a good wife," he predicted. "Always meat on the table."

"And I want some of it right now," she declared energetically, and headed for the kitchen.

Webb tapped his wounded arm. "Got a notion you sorta evened up for this punctured flipper of mine," he observed. "Must have been the same bunch, don't you think?"

"Logical to presume so," Slade replied. "I certainly hope so; can do without two of that calibre mavericking around."

"You're darn right," growled Webb. "One is more than plenty. 'Pears the blasted section gets worse all the time instead of better."

"Eventually it will quiet down, but not for a while, I fear," Slade answered. "Sanderson is still a focal point for the lawless of the Big Bend country and the trans-Pecos region to the west. And the rangeland is vulnerable, to an extent, where widelooping activities are concerned, with the hills to the north and the Rio Grande curving up this way on the south."

Webb nodded gloomily and insisted on filling his pipe without assistance.

"There, she's all loaded," he announced. He fumbled a match, flipped it alight with his thumbnail and applied the flame.

"Some good from having a flipper outa shape," he chuckled between puffs. "Teaches you how well you can get along with just one." He took a long and triumphant drag and blew out the smoke.

"Come and get it or I'll throw it away," sounded Mary's voice from the kitchen.

"I et a little while ago," Webb said. "Go ahead, son, and feed your tapeworm."

Slade shook hands with Miguel, the Mexican cook, and complimented him on what he had dished up on such short notice.

"Prepared already I was," replied Miguel, with a low bow. "El Halcon, the good, the just, the friend of the lowly, must not be kept waiting."

"Thank you, Miguel," Slade said soberly. "I am honored." Miguel beamed.

"Always, dear, you say just the right thing," Mary murmured as they sat down. "It's a gift!"

They showed full appreciation of Miguel's offering, with the appetite of youth and perfect digestion. Mary remained in the kitchen to help clean up. Slade rejoined Webb in the big, luxuriously furnished living room.

"Met your new neighbor on our way up," he observed.

"Hale," Webb nodded. "Seems to be a purty nice sort of a jigger. Good cowman, too. Got that old spread going in first-class shape in a hurry. We could do with more like him."

"Know where he came from?" Slade asked.

"Over around the Red River country, I heard," Webb replied.

"Rather indefinite," Slade smiled. "The old Red is a lot of river. More than six hundred miles through or along the boundary of Texas."

"Yep, she is," Webb agreed. "That's all I know of where he came from. Don't remember him mentioning any more than that. I rode up to his place when he first took over the Rockin' L, to be neighborly. Seemed to appreciate the visit. Dropped in here a couple of times. Asked a lot of questions about the section and the folks here, which wasn't surprising. Speaks well."

"Yes, he does," Slade replied thoughtfully. "A man of some education, I'd say. Has an accent that seemed to me more Louisiana than Texas. Nothing unusual about that, however. A lot of folks, especially cattlemen, have crossed the Sabine and settled here."

"Uh-huh, that's so," said Webb. "I know a coupla jiggers who did just that. Well, everybody knows that for cow country, Texas can't be beat."

Mary joined them and the subject of Griswold Hale was dropped for the time being.

For a couple of hours they sat and chatted about ranch matters and the carting business. From time to time, old John gazed longingly at the rangeland glowing in the reddish rays of the low-lying sun. Finally he said,

"Walt, how about taking a little ride? I haven't been out since I was plugged and I'm getting mighty tired of being cooped up. Guess I can take a chance of being shot at again."

"I don't think you'd be taking much of a chance with Walt along," Mary put in as Slade hesitated. "Trying to drygulch him is a chore, usually a fatal one for the drygulcher."

"Guess you've got something there, chick," Webb agreed. "What say, Walt, let's go."

8

A wrangler saddled Webb's horse. Slade got the rig on Shadow and they set out.

"Short-cut through the canyons?" Webb asked.

"No," Slade decided at once. "We follow the open trail that curves around the eastern base of the hills, where I can keep a watch on things."

"You figure these devils might be layin' fer us?" said Webb.

"I don't know," Slade admitted, "but after what's been happening of late, I'm prepared for anything."

Webb nodded and they rode on, the rancher expounding on the condition of the stock they passed. Slade, however, was mostly silent, his eyes constantly sweeping the crests of the rises. The slopes were but thinly brush-grown, but on the crests the chaparral was quite dense. They had covered but a couple of miles when he suddenly pulled Shadow to a halt and sat gazing at the crest some little distance ahead. Webb shot him an inquiring look.

"Somebody up top that sag, probably keeping tabs on us," Slade said.

"How do you know?" Webb asked. "I can't see anything."

"Look close," Slade told him. "See that little

dot rising and falling over the brush? That's a bluejay. More than once those little fussy jiggers have done me a good turn. There's something near his nest or his perch that bothers him."

"Coyote, snake?" Webb hazarded. Slade shook his head.

"Coyotes don't batten on bluejays," he replied. "And he'd peck the eyes out of a snake that came too close. No, it's something else, something he doesn't understand and fears. All right, turn to the left and keep riding."

Webb did so and for a while they rode east, by a little south, Slade constantly scanning the crest of the slope, estimating the distance from their position to the crest. Now they were opposite where the jay still sweeped and fluttered.

"Better than six hundred yards," Slade remarked. "This should do it. We should be fairly safe here, and my rifle is sighted almost point-blank at a thousand yards. Yes, there's some hellion up there. I'll see if I can smoke him out."

He drew the big rifle from the saddle boot and flung it forward, holding a bit high. The muzzle belched smoke and flame.

"That should serve notice we have caught on to him," he remarked. "Chances are he'll hightail in a hurry."

However, "he" didn't. There was the distant clang of a report and a slug whined by overhead.

"Want to play rough, eh?" Slade said, his face

setting in grim lines. “Loco hellion should know I’ve got him outranged.

“Not doing too bad, though,” he added, as another bullet passed by, closer.

But now El Halcon had spotted the wisp of smoke that rose from the brush. The Winchester cut loose with a rattling roar, three shots almost as one.

The growth at the lip of the crest was violently agitated. Something pitched into view, rolled over and over down the slope to come to rest motionless.

“Keep behind your horse’s neck,” Slade warned the rancher. “Could be another one up there.”

His gaze alternated from the form on the slope to the crest. Nothing happened; the silence remained unbroken save for the diminishing notes of the jay, which reached El Halcon’s ears. Another moment and the bird had settled into the chaparral.

“Guess that’s all, but you stay right where you are,” he ordered old John. “No, I don’t want you with me; you’d just be in the way. Stay put.”

With which he sent Shadow pacing slowly toward the base of the slope, leaning well sideways in the saddle.

The hilltop remained peaceful. He reached the slope and rode up the sag. He slowed the horse when he passed the body of the drygulcher, but spared it only a glance. A hard-case looking devil with nothing outstanding about him, so far as Slade could see.

Still without untoward incident, he topped the sag and pushed his way into the denser growth.

As he expected, he found a horse tethered to a branch. He removed the rig and left the animal where it was. Turning back to the slope, he beckoned a reassuring hand to Webb, who immediately rode forward to join him, appearing little disturbed by the affair.

Slade dismounted beside the drygulcher's body and gave it a closer examination. Just another "hired hand" who obeyed orders but showed poor judgment; that was Slade's verdict. The pockets revealed nothing of importance save some money, which he replaced. Up the slope a little ways, he spotted the fellow's rifle, a regulation arm. Retrieving it, he dropped it beside the body, mounted and rode down the sag to where Webb awaited him.

"Persistent devils," he remarked as he joined the rancher. "Don't appear to have any intention of letting up."

"I think this time they were after you, not me," Webb said. "Guess they figured you'd be riding back to town this way."

"It is possible," Slade conceded. He thought Webb had the right notion.

"Son, that was sure some shooting you did," the rancher said admiringly. "Close to seven hundred yards. If I hadn't seen it, I wouldn't have believed it."

"It's a good iron," Slade replied smilingly as he refilled the magazine. Webb gave a derisive snort.

"Yep, Mary had the right of it," he said. "Trying to drygulch El Halcon is just a nice fast way to commit suicide."

Slade laughed, and did not argue the point. For some moments he sat gazing south to where the rangeland ran down to the Rio Grande, with several good fords handy. A very convenient arrangement for the rustlers. But it might also provide opportunity to law enforcement officers. He turned to Webb.

"Well, wish to keep on riding?"

"Nope," the rancher replied. "I wanta go home. Soon be dark and I'll be seein' owlhoots behind every tree."

Slade glanced up the slope as they got under way, and chuckled.

"Another packing-in chore for Tom Crane," he observed. "He'll be fit to be hogtied when he hears about it."

"I'll send a couple of the boys to notify him," Webb offered. "Young hellions will be glad of a chance to spend a night in town."

"A good notion," Slade agreed. "Then he can ride up first thing in the morning and have time to pay a visit."

Mary Merril wasn't exactly fit to be hogtied when they arrived at the ranchhouse and informed her of what had happened, but she wasn't far from it. She shook her curly head resignedly.

"I'm not surprised," she said to Slade. "You couldn't walk around the barn without getting into some sort of a mix-up. How do you feel, Uncle John?"

"A heck of a sight better," Webb replied. "Seein' one of those sidewinders laid out stiff did me a whale of a lot of good. Guess the ornery galoots are beginning to understand what it means to lock horns with El Halcon. Gentlemen, hush!"

"I'm hungry again," Mary announced.

"So am I," replied Webb. "Lookin' at dead owlhoots whets up my appetite."

"I hope you don't develop cannibalistic tendencies," replied his niece.

"Oh, a slice of owlhoot, fried in butter, might not be too bad," old John rejoined cheerfully.

"Ugh!" said Mary. "Let's talk about something else!"

After they had finished eating and the kitchen was cleaned up, Mary gently but firmly led Slade to her fine grand piano. She spoke no words, but the action spoke louder than words. Slade smiled, adjusted the stool to his liking and sat down, running his slender fingers over the keys with crisp power.

“Wait!” exclaimed old John. “Wait till I fetch the boys and the cook.”

He hurried out and soon returned with the Cross W hands streaming after him. Mary already had old Miguel, the cook, in a chair beside her.

Slade smiled at his expectant audience and sang, his great golden baritone-bass filling the room with melody.

Songs the cowboys loved. Songs of the horse and the dog and the men who loved both. Songs of the sun-drenched rangeland, the peaceful stars, the lonely campfires and the sleeping herds.

His voice thundering and pealing like the Rio Grande in its sunken gorge, then soft as the fall of the summer rain, whispering notes of glorious sound. And last, a poignantly wistful love song of old *Mejico* which caused Miguel to smile tremulously and dewed Mary’s lashes with the glitter of tears.

The piano roared forth crashing chords, stilled, and Slade flashed at his enrapt hearers the white smile of El Halcon that men—and women—found irresistible, and rose to his splendid height, standing for a moment in his youth and strength like a tall pine of the forest.

“Well,” sighed Joyce Echols, “makes me almost wish I’d lived a better life.”

“If that is so,” old John said firmly, “the day of miracles ain’t past!”

The cowboys filed out. Joyce Echols turned to El Halcon.

"Going to have a little session of poker in the bunkhouse, Mr. Slade," he said. "Like to set in for a hand or two?"

"Don't mind if I do," Slade accepted.

Mary made a face at him. But she was still curled up in a chair in the living room, waiting, when he returned.

The sheriff and his deputies arrived at the ranchhouse shortly before noon, leading the dead drygulcher's horse, the body strapped to the back of a pack mule. Crane was in a better temper than Slade had anticipated.

"Figured we'd drop in for a bite and a gabfast before heading to town," he said. "You going to ride back with us, Walt?"

"Yes, I think I shall," Slade replied. "Everything quiet in town?"

"Oh, sure, except for a ruckus in that blasted rumhole on Railroad Street, the Big Enough," the sheriff answered. "Nothing serious."

"George Tumulty's place?"

"Tumulty don't own it anymore," growled Crane. "He sold out a while back to a rowdy galoot named Foster, Blaine Foster. The crowd Tumulty used to get was bad enough, but the bunch Foster gets is worse. Younger cowhands and railroaders and carters, and some others the devil alone knows what they are. Been several shindigs there the past couple of months, since Foster took over. Foster is a big feller and salty, though, and so far has managed to keep things sorta in hand, but I'm expecting real trouble there, sooner or later. Figure Foster used to be a cowhand. Rides around a lot and sometimes don't show up for two or three days."

"Was he in the saloon business elsewhere?" Slade asked.

"Couldn't say for sure," the sheriff said. "He don't say much about himself. Gather he came here from Arizona; figure he's been around plenty. Talks like a educated feller."

"I see," Slade nodded, his eyes thoughtful.

"Now suppose you give me the real lowdown on what happened yesterday," Crane suggested.

Webb obliged, in detail.

"So you played 'em aces-back-to-back per usual," the sheriff commented to Slade when the rancher paused.

"The bluejay deserves most of the credit, for showing me where the devil was holed up," Slade said.

"I'd never have paid any attention to the little coot and, the chances are, got myself shot because I didn't," remarked Webb.

"Learn to study the ways of the birds and the beasts of the wild," Slade advised. "They'll be your friends if you'll just give them the chance.

Their actions tell a story as plain as the printed page, if one learns to read them aright. Many's the time they've saved me from trouble."

After a bountiful snack and a smoke, the sheriff announced his intention of heading for town.

"I'll try and get back tomorrow or next day," Slade told Mary.

"Don't bother to, my dear," she replied over her shoulder as she trotted up the stairs. "I'm going along. I want another night in town and I'd like to see that nice place Uncle Tom spoke of—the Big Enough."

"You would!" Slade groaned. "Sometimes I think you dote on looking for trouble."

"But I'm not bad to have along when there is trouble," she pointed out.

The truth of which Slade was forced to admit.

"Might have knowed she had something in mind when she put on her riding duds this morning," remarked Webb. "Well, she's twenty-one and her own boss; nothing I can do about it."

"And a darn good businesswoman," observed the sheriff.

9

Mary was back downstairs in a couple of minutes, bearing a bundle she stowed in her saddle pouch.

The trip was slow but uneventful and they reached Sanderson just at sunset. Mary at once headed for her hotel room, with her bundle.

"I'll be in the Branding Pen in an hour or so," she told Slade.

He cared for her horse and Shadow. Then he and the sheriff repaired to the latter's office, where the body had already been laid out on the floor, with the deputies in attendance.

The usual crowd of the curious drifted in to view the remains, with no important results. This time even Deputy Ester did not recall having seen the fellow in life.

After a bit, Crane shooed out the stragglers and locked the door, the deputies having departed in quest of refreshment. He and Slade proceeded to talk things over.

"Anyhow the little imp gave me a good excuse for visiting the Big Enough," Slade chuckled. "I feel sort of interested in the place."

"Thought you would be," said Crane. "That's why I spoke of it as I did. The row in there last night was really not worth mentioning. I'll admit I've been a mite curious about it, too. Some very shady-looking characters hang out in there. And I figure any newcomer to the section is worth keeping an eye on till we learn something about him."

"That's right," Slade agreed. "We are in the unpleasant position of having nobody to really suspect, which makes everybody suspect who appears to in the least qualify.

"But don't prejudge Foster and his crowd," he warned. "Being rowdy and quarrelsome doesn't necessarily mean they are guilty of anything really off-color. Surface appearances can be deceptive, as you well know. Remember Fletcher Bartlett and his Diamond F bunch of rowdy hands. You looked sideways at them for quite a while and they turned out to be just a bunch of turbulent young jiggers with a penchant for kicking up rows when they had a few snorts of redeye under their belts."

"Guess that's so," Crane admitted. "Reckon all we can do is keep our eyes open."

"Exactly," Slade said. "Our really important chore at the moment is to try and figure where the outlaws are most likely to strike next. I've a notion what happened last night on the cliff top will set them back a bit, but not for long. I think they had a chore of widelooping in mind when they ran into Joyce Echols. It didn't work out, and right now they are probably suffering from a lack of spending money, a condition no owlhoot leader can afford to have prevail for long, if he hopes to keep his men in line. So once again we'll do a little pondering and see if we can come up with something."

"Right," said Crane. "Think-tank work in order."

"By the way," Slade remarked, "I met another newcomer as Mary and I were riding to the ranchhouse; Griswold Hale."

"Uh-huh," said the sheriff. "Bought the Rocking L spread a few months back. You'll rec'lect it was for sale. Didn't change the registered brand and kept on the Rocking L riders. They're mostly old jiggers who had been with Tolliver, the former owner, for a long time. Guess they were glad not to have to trail their twine to new diggin's. Good hands, maybe a mite slow, but they know how to get the work done and know the section."

Slade mentioned the matter of the artesian wells Hale proposed to drill.

"Yep, he's got notions, all right," Crane said. "The Rocking L casa sets on a rise, and down at the bottom of the rise is a big spring. Hale built a tank on top of the house and down at the spring he put a thing-a-ma-jig he calls a hydraulic ram or something like that. It pumps water into the tank, so he's got running water in the house. I don't know how the darn thing works, but it does."

"Really a quite simple device," Slade explained. "The water is conducted from the spring to the ram through a straight, smooth inclined pipe offering little resistance to the flow. A valve opens downward through which the water at first escapes; as the speed of the water increases, the valve is closed by pressure. The sudden stopping of the stream causes a great pressure at the end of the pipe in consequence of the forward momentum of the stream; under this pressure the valve opens upward and water is forced into the pipe leading to the tank on the roof, and the dome of the ram, slightly compressing the air in the dome. When the momentum of the water is spent, the reaction closes the valve to the dome and opens the valve to the spring feed pipe. Water again flows out at the spring pipe valve with increasing velocity until it is closed and water is again driven through the tank pipe by the hammer-like blow of the column of water in the spring pipe. This cycle of operation continues indefinitely, water being gradually forced up the tank pipe until it may reach many times the height through which the stream falls, pouring into the tank on the roof. The air chamber in the upper half of the dome is essential as it furnishes an elastic cushion with but little inertia, enabling the spring valve to close instantly.

"That's really all there is to it. The hydraulic ram in operation is about as near perpetual motion as man has been able so far to evolve."

"Sounds fine," the sheriff commented dryly, "but I still can't figure how the blasted thing works."

Slade laughed and switched to another topic, that of trying to out-guess the next move of the mysterious and elusive outlaw bunch.

"The devils are sure after you hot and heavy," Crane remarked. "Three tries so far."

"And three failures," Slade replied, with a smile. "In one way, good comes from it. While they are concentrating on me, they are not pulling something on somebody else."

"Just fine again!" snorted the sheriff, "like teasin' a snake—hasn't got time to bite anybody else, but what if he fangs you?"

"The idea," said Slade, "is to keep making him miss his stroke."

The sheriff's reaction to this decidedly caustic philosophy was another and more explosive snort.

Although Slade felt the session had been futile, with no definite results, it broke up on a cheerful note. Things would work out; they always did.

"Suppose we amble over to the Branding Pen," Crane suggested. "Your gal had oughta be there by now."

She was. And overalls and shirt had been replaced by a very modish, and, Slade thought, very becoming costume.

"So that's what you had in the bundle," he remarked.

"Well, you can't expect a girl to show up in a new place the first time in overalls and a shirt," she replied.

"Still hanker for a look at the Big Enough, eh?"

"Uh-huh, and a look at that terrible and ferocious Mr. Foster Uncle Tom told us about. Bet he turns out to be real nice."

"Some folks have a liking for wildcats and grizzly bears," grunted the sheriff. "Let us drink!"

Which they proceeded to do while waiting for their dinner to be prepared. The sheriff turned to Mary.

"Packin' your gun along?" he asked.

"I trust I won't need it," she replied obliquely. The sheriff chuckled.

"If you do, maybe we'll catch on to how you pull it without anybody seeing where it come from," he predicted hopefully.

"You won't," the girl declared flatly. Crane chuckled again.

"Folks say Walt is the fastest gunhand in the whole dadblamed Southwest," he remarked meditatively. "But sometimes I wonder just a mite."

Mary made a face at him and changed the subject.

They enjoyed a leisurely dinner, chatted with

Hardrock for a while. Then, after another drink for the sheriff and a final cup of coffee for Slade, Mary jumped to her feet.

"Now I want to go to the Big Enough," she announced. "Don't worry, Mr. Hogan, we won't neglect you. It's just that I'm always curious about any place Uncle Tom looks sideways at. Usually a disappointment, though; turns out to be tiresomely tame."

They reached the Big Enough without incident; it was on Railroad Street, across from the boom and bustle of the yards. When they entered, Slade at once noted that the lighting had been improved, and that the furnishings were new and in good taste.

"There's Foster down at the end of the bar," the sheriff remarked. Slade surveyed the Big Enough owner with interest.

Blaine Foster was a tall man, powerfully built. His hair was almost as black as Slade's own, and he had snapping black eyes. Slade judged his age to be between thirty-five and forty, probably nearer the latter figure. He hurried forward, smiling broadly, to greet the group.

"Well, well, this is an honor!" he boomed while still half a dozen paces distant, with a frankly admiring glance at Mary.

Sheriff Crane performed the introductions. Foster bowed over Mary's hand, shook with Slade. He had a powerful grip and evidently liked to use it, but when their hands fell apart, there were white rings around his fingers. He shot the Ranger a look of respect.

The sheriff stifled a grin. "Tried to grip with El Halcon, eh?" he murmured to himself. "Guess you'll know better next time."

Foster led them to a table near the dance floor, beckoned a waiter.

"Everything on the house," he directed. He crinkled his eyes at Slade.

"Got to keep on the good side of the Law," he explained. "Never can tell when I might need him. Some of my boys get a mite proddy now and then."

Studying the crowd a moment, Slade felt it was probably so. They were, for the most part, devil-may-care young fellows from the spreads and the railroad, ready for anything that promised excitement. But, aside from a few individuals he had not yet definitely classified, with no real harm in them. On these last, he reserved judgment until he possibly knew more about them. They struck him as being of the "passing through" variety that always attracted the Ranger's attention.

"Name your pizen, folks," Foster said jovially. "Mind if I sit with you a while?"—regarding Mary.

"Please do, Mr. Foster," she replied. Slade and the sheriff seconded the invitation.

Foster proved to be a good conversationalist,

his choice of words excellent. Slade quickly concluded he had been around plenty.

The orchestra, which could really play, began a dreamy waltz.

"I want to dance," Mary said. Foster glanced at Slade.

"May I?" he asked diffidently.

"If the lady confers," Slade replied, with a smile.

"The lady confers," Mary laughed. "Come on, Mr. Foster."

"Big fellow can dance, all right," Crane remarked a moment later.

"Yes, he can," Slade agreed. "Very light on his feet for so big a man."

The sheriff chuckled softly as he glanced at Mary, and noted that Foster's lips were moving.

"If there's anything to learn about him, she'll learn it," he predicted.

"Yes, she will," Slade agreed. "She's smart as a whip and has a knack for making people talk."

They had two numbers together; then Foster brought her back to the table, rosy and breathless, for the second number had been a fast one.

"Have to leave you for a few minutes," he apologized and hurried to the far end of the bar, where his head drink juggler was yelping for stock.

"Well?" Slade asked.

"Oh, sure, I persuaded him to talk about

himself," Mary replied. "That's why I danced with him, as you very well know. His father owns a ranch in the Animas Valley in Arizona. But there are three younger brothers and he decided to set out on his own. Chuck line rider for a while, visited California, Oregon, New Mexico. Back to Arizona. Got a job dealing cards in a Tucson saloon. Saved his money. Concluded the saloon business was easier and more lucrative than ranching. Bought a share in the saloon where he worked. Saved more money. Heard a lot about Texas and decided there was better opportunity here. Jumped at the chance to buy the Big Enough. Says he's here to stay, that it is an up-and-coming section and figures he should do well. I expect he will. Isn't married and never has been. Said he's afraid of women, which I think is the only untruth he told. How did I do?"

"Wonderfully," Slade applauded. "Learned more in half an hour than I would have been able to in a month."

"A woman can usually get a man to talk, especially about himself," Mary said demurely.

"Especially under the right conditions; don't I know!" Slade voiced positive agreement.

The sheriff roared with laughter. Mary blushed.

"What do you think, Walt?" Crane asked.

"Sounds like a straight story," Slade replied. "Gaps in it, however. Mary, did he happen to mention how long since he left his father's ranch?"

"Yes, come to think of it, he did," the girl replied. "Said it was seven years since he'd been home, except for a couple of short visits after he returned to Arizona."

"A man can be a lot of places and do a lot of things in seven years," Slade said thoughtfully. "He must have saved a good deal of money to buy this place and refurnish it as he has. Of course, though, dealers are usually good card players, and he could have sat in games when not working and tied onto considerable dinero that way; has been done. And there is and always has been a lot of loose money floating around Tucson. A really good card player might win quite a poke in a short time. That could be the answer to his apparent affluence when he coiled his twine here. So we'll have to give amigo Foster a clean bill of health until we have reason to think otherwise."

"Guess so," grumbled the sheriff. "But I still figure the hellions he gets in here are capable of anything."

"A saloon owner can't pick and choose his clientele," Slade pointed out. "Even the Branding Pen gets some characters Hardrock would prefer to see conspicuous for their absence. But so long as they behave themselves, he can hardly ask them to stay away. The same applies to Foster."

"Uh-huh, but birds of a feather herd up in the same bunch," said the sheriff, slightly misquoting an old adage.

"Yes," Slade agreed smilingly, "but a hen can hatch a nest of duck eggs, and although the results drive her loco, there isn't anything she can do but put up with them."

"A rather far-fetched parallel, but it does apply," Mary remarked. "I want another glass of wine."

Foster insisted on remedying that lack himself, and had one with her.

Slade sat with his gaze fixed on the bar, where two groups of cowhands were wrangling; he watched them closely.

Foster had just emptied his glass when the row cut loose, and it was a good one. Instantly one whole section of the bar was a hitting, wrestling, scuffling tangle. Foster leaped to his feet and rushed to the bar, between the two groups, hurling men right and left.

"Stay where you are," Slade snapped to Mary and glided close to the scene of hostilities.

Steel gleamed. A knife poised behind Foster's back. But before the forward thrust was completed, fingers like rods of nickel steel closed on the wielder's wrist. He screamed in agony as El Halcon's awful grip ground his wrist bones together. The knife fell from his hand.

Slade caught it with his right hand before it hit the floor, flipped it. The razor-sharp point pricked the fellow's throat.

In the same flicker of movement he let go the knife man's wrist, snapped the blade in two and cast the pieces aside; seized the other by the shirt front.

"Stop it! That's enough!" he thundered to the cowhands.

When El Halcon spoke in that tone, men obeyed. The two groups drew apart, sullenly, staring at him. Holding the still moaning knife man helpless, Slade spoke, his voice soft and musical, but deadly.

"Get out," he said. "And it would be a good notion not to come back."

The man glared up at him, but the eyes boring into his were the terrible eyes of El Halcon. He cringed.

Slade gave him a shove toward the door. He lurched out and disappeared.

"What I want to know," said one of the cowhands, rubbing his side, "is why somebody hit me a kidney punch when my back was turned. Who was it?"

"He just left," Slade replied.

"But why did he do it?" persisted the waddie. "I never saw him before in my life. I thought it was one of those Lazy H hellions. Why did he do it?"

"So you loco jugheads would start a ruckus and set the stage for a murder," Slade replied. "It very nearly worked. Now get back to the bar and behave yourselves."

He turned, to face two guns.

10

One was held by Sheriff Crane, the other by Mary Merril.

"Why'd you let him go?" demanded the sheriff. "I'd have thrown the blankety-blank in the calaboose."

"Tell you later," Slade replied, and led the way back to the table.

"And I still didn't see how she pulled it, or where from, and how she got rid of it again!" wailed Crane. Mary giggled.

"You don't need to know," she said. "I want some more wine."

With peace restored, Foster rejoined them a few minutes later. His face had a strained look.

"Guess you saved me from getting that sticker in my back, Mr. Slade," he said slowly.

"Possibly," the Ranger conceded, and beckoned the waiter to bring coffee.

"No 'possibly' about it," Foster declared emphatically. "Were it not for you, right now I'd be a dead man. Well, I won't forget it."

Foster returned to the end of the bar for a moment, to confer with his head bartender. The sheriff turned to Slade.

"Why *did* that sidewinder try to murder Foster?" he asked.

"I wish I knew for sure," Slade replied thoughtfully.

"And why did you let him go?"

"Because," Slade explained, "I'll know him if I see him again; he might lead us to somebody. I feel fairly certain that attempt at a killing was not his own idea. He did play it smart, though. Saw opportunity and took advantage of it in a very shrewd and daring manner. A long ways from being terrapin-brained."

"Nobody 'pears to rec'lect seeing him before," Crane commented. " 'Pears he was a stranger."

"I believe," Slade said, "that he was one of the pair that escaped during the fight on the cliff top by Echo Canyon. Short but massively built. I couldn't swear to it, but I believe he was."

"I still think you should have let me drop a loop on him," the sheriff grumbled. "Could have booked him for attempted murder."

"Tying onto a 'hired hand' could get us little," Slade pointed out. "Whereas running around loose, he might prove of definite value. I'm convinced now that a well-organized bunch with a very shrewd devil at the head of it is operating in the section. What we want is the big he-wolf of the pack. With him corralled, the outfit would quickly fall apart. Well, we'll see."

"Think you broke the devil's arm?" Crane asked.

"I doubt it," Slade answered. "I didn't twist; just put the pressure on."

"Which was plenty," said the sheriff. "One thing's sure for certain, he'll have a darn sore wrist for a while. Doubt if he'll go in for any knife work for some time to come."

"He handled a blade almost like a Yaqui-Mexican knife man," Slade observed thoughtfully. "Aimed to use an upward thrust that nobody would hardly notice. Foster would have toppled over and during the ensuing excitement he'd have slid out before anybody realized what had actually happened."

"How'd you catch on so fast?" Crane asked.

"I was watching those cowhands," Slade explained. "I felt they were going to start a shindig. I saw that fellow slide in behind one and throw the punch at his back. He had been taking no part in the argument and evidently did not belong to either group. So I thought it a rather queer thing for him to do, and when he pulled the blade I was ready for him."

"Darn lucky for Foster you were," grunted Crane.

Foster rejoined them at that moment. "Sorry it had to happen with you present, Miss Merril," he said. "I hope you were not too disturbed."

"Not at all," Mary returned. "Don't worry about me. Really, I enjoyed it, so long as nobody was seriously hurt."

Foster gave her a frankly admiring glance. "I believe you really did," he said.

"Familiarity breeds contempt, you know," Mary answered. "Stick around with Walt and excitement is of such frequent occurrence one quickly learns to treat it as a matter of course. No lack of action when you are in his company."

"You're darn right," said Crane. "It just nacherly follows him around, and if there ain't none handy, he manages to stir up a little himself."

Foster laughed, and suggested another drink, which the sheriff accepted. Slade settled for a final cup of coffee. Mary declined.

"Have to watch my complexion," she explained.

"You must have been watching it very carefully for a long time," the saloon owner declared.

"I'm beginning to think, Mr. Foster, that you have the same gift for blarney as Walt," the girl rejoined. "He makes one believe it against one's better judgment," she added with a little sigh.

"I can't get over the way he handled the situation," Foster said. "A word from him and those cowhands did just as he told them to."

"Which goes to show they've got more brains than you might give 'em credit of having," the sheriff observed dryly. "Of course, some of 'em know him, and know better'n to arg'fy with El Halcon. Do as he tells you and stay healthy."

"Really he's not as terrible a person as Uncle Tom tries to make him out to be," Mary protested. "Have you any Mexicans in your employ, Mr. Foster?"

"Why, yes, all my kitchen help are Mexicans," Foster replied. "They're tops at that work."

"Ask them about El Halcon," the girl advised. "They'll give you the straight story. That reminds me, speaking of the kitchen, I'm hungry again."

"Here we go!" groaned the sheriff. "Pounds and pounds! Those jiggers will know he is here, and I'll wager they're already throwing together something special. Eat with him, and you don't have to watch your waistline, 'cause you ain't got any."

Foster laughed heartily and hurried to the kitchen, where he remained for some little time. When he returned, he wore a slightly bewildered look. Mary smiled, but asked no questions.

The snack, as Foster termed it, was soon forthcoming, and it was all the sheriff predicted it would be. He proceeded to forget all about waistlines. So did the others, for that matter, including Foster himself, who elected to join them.

After they finished eating, Slade stood up.

"Mr. Foster," he said, "if you don't mind, I'd like to go back to the kitchen and thank the boys."

"Go right ahead," Foster instantly agreed. "It will please them."

Slade chatted with the kitchen help for some minutes in his flawless Spanish, and left them smiling happily.

"How few would think of doing that," Foster marveled to Mary as they awaited his return.

"Yes," the girl said. "Always he remembers. Always he thinks of the lowly."

"I only hope," Foster said, and his voice shook slightly as he said it, "that someday somebody will say of me what the kitchen boys said of him. Indeed it is something to be likened to Our Lord."

Mary glanced at the clock when Slade rejoined them, smiled brightly at Foster.

"Really I think we should be going back to the Branding Pen, before Mr. Hogan begins to think we have deserted him," she said. "And thank you very much, Mr. Foster, for a most enjoyable evening."

"I'm sure happy to hear you say it," Foster replied. "And please come again."

"We will," Mary promised. "I like your place, and I'm sure Walt and Uncle Tom do also. Perhaps you will be able to provide us with more entertainment next time."

"I think I can do with a little less of that sort," Foster replied, a bit grimly.

As they walked back to the Branding Pen, the sheriff said to Slade,

"Well, what do you think?"

"Frankly, I don't know what to think," El Halcon answered.

"He's a good deal of a puzzler, and what happened tonight was also quite puzzling, too; seemed so senseless."

"Owlhoots sometimes fall out among themselves," the sheriff observed sententiously.

"Yes," Slade conceded, "but that presupposes something relative to Blaine Foster for which we have no basis of fact."

Crane grunted but refrained from further discussing the matter.

"Well, here we are," he remarked as they pushed through the swinging doors. "Crowded and noisy, per usual."

Old Hardrock came forward to escort them to their table.

"Well, how'd you like the Big Enough?" he asked.

"We liked it fine," Mary replied. "Nice and exciting."

She immediately launched into a vivid account of what had happened there, the sheriff interpolating a word now and then. Hardrock gazed at Slade and shook his bristly head.

"He just nacherly takes everybody in; that is, everybody of the right sort," was his comment.

"Uh-huh, and them of the wrong sort he 'takes in' too, in a different way," the sheriff said.

"Guess that's so," Hardrock agreed. "Like that

wind spider who tried to kill Foster. Got a notion he's feelin' sorta took in about now."

"Hello!" Mary exclaimed. "There's Mr. Griswold Hale at the bar."

"Yep, he comes in now and then, not too often," Hardrock said. "Guess he's purty busy getting his holding in shape. Nice quiet feller. Never has much to say but always pleasant to everybody. He's lookin' this way."

"Call him over, Tom," Slade suggested.

The sheriff did so. Hale sauntered across to the table, his stride lithe and graceful, accepted a chair and a drink.

"Got my drilling rig, Mr. Slade," he said, after a few words of greeting. "Hope to get operating in a day or two. Ride up to my place if you can find the time. I've a notion you would be able to give me some pointers."

"I'll try and make it soon," Slade promised. In fact, he had already decided to pay a visit to the Rocking L in the near future.

They chatted for a while, about ranching and other matters dealing with the section. Hale offered to buy a round of drinks.

Slade and Mary declined, explaining they'd already had their quota. The sheriff decided to have a last one to keep him company.

When the glasses were empty, Hale glanced at the clock and rose to his feet.

"Sorry to part with congenial company, but I

must get some sleep," he said. "Got a busy day ahead of me."

With a smile and a nod, he departed. Mary's eyes followed his tall form to the door, a little pucker between her delicate black brows. Slade regarded her thoughtfully and the concentration furrow between his own brows deepened a trifle.

"Well," said Crane, "I vote we call it a night; been a darn busy one and I craves shut-eye. No telling what may bust loose tomorrow."

"And I expect to have a conference with Pancho Arista about the carting business," said Mary. "I too am in favor of calling it a night. How about you, Walt?"

"I vote with the majority," El Halcon smiled.

After saying goodnight to Hardrock, they left the Branding Pen, which, although the hour was late, was still busy and noisy.

"Doc will hold an inquest on that varmint we packed in a bit after noon, according to his plans, but he'll wait till John Webb gets here," the sheriff said when they parted. "Figure John to be the only witness. Anyhow, he's itchin' for an excuse to come to town."

11

Shortly before noon, Webb arrived, feeling quite chipper, even though his arm was still in a sling. The inquest got under way on schedule and was the usual humdrum monotony with the usual results. Court adjourned, and the coroner, his jury, and Webb repaired to the Branding Pen to recover from their exhausting labors. The body was packed off to Sanderson's fast-growing Boot Hill. Sheriff Crane contemplated the empty floor.

"Don't look right with nothing on it," he remarked to Slade. "Well, won't be that way long, I predict."

"A nice optimistic viewpoint," Slade replied. "Hope you're right. That is, if they are of the same calibre as the latest occupant. And that, incidentally, is the contingency that bothers me most, that again some innocent individual may be murdered in the course of one of their depredations."

"Yes, that's something to really worry about," Crane agreed. "And blast it! We still don't know for sure who to look for. Walt, I'm asking you straight, do you figure for sure Blaine Foster ain't our man?"

"I'm not yet ready to definitely discard Foster as a suspect," Slade replied. "He tells a straight story, appears to be sincere. But as I said last night, there are gaps in the story, he told Mary. Undoubtedly there were years during which he made no mention of his activities, merely intimating that during that period he was a chuck line rider. Of course a wandering cowhand can put in a lot of time doing nothing of any consequence, but somehow it is hard to vision Foster living that sort of a life for years. He is an intelligent individual, gives the appearance of being ambitious and a square shooter. Which, conceding that he is a person of well above average intelligence, is of course the impression he would strive to give, if there is anything off-color about him. And still unexplained is why a cunning and unsavory-appearing hellion would try to kill him.

"So there you have it relative to *amigo* Foster; nothing but rather vague theorizing. I'll sound out Mary a little and learn what her feminine intuition has to say; I've learned to put dependence in it.

"However, I'll honestly admit that I'm not overly hopeful where Blaine Foster is concerned, so far."

"And there's where *your* 'intuition' you call a hunch is edging into the picture," growled Crane. "First you build up a real nice case against him, then you hand it a knockout wallop. Oh, why didn't I stick to followin' a cow's tail 'stead of gettin' mixed up in politics and this blasted sheriffin' business!"

Slade laughed and stood up, stretching his long arms over his head.

"I'm going out to walk a little bit," he announced. "Then I'll meet Mary at the Branding Pen. She's riding to the spread with Webb, a little later. Joyce Echols and a couple more of the Cross W hands are accompanying them; she'll be back tomorrow evening."

In the course of his walk, Slade visited the carting station, where Webb and Arista carts were lined up, tarpaulins in place to protect the loads against bad weather. Looked like they were all set to roll.

Neither Mary nor Pancho Arista were present, so a little later Slade repaired to the Branding Pen, where he found the girl awaiting him.

"Have your confab with Arista?" he asked as he sat down.

"Yes, we got together and made plans," she replied.

"Passed by the station and saw your carts appeared to be loaded and ready to go," he remarked. Mary glanced around, lowered her voice.

"Walt, they're not loaded," she said. "Although they give the appearance of being loaded, they're empty and will be, save for money, quite a lot of it, that will be hid beneath feed sacks in the lead cart. They'll be empty so they'll travel fast. They'll be headed for Marathon, where they'll pick up a valuable cargo that came up from the south and must be paid for on delivery."

"I see," El Halcon said. "All set to roll in the morning, then."

Mary again glanced around, and lowered her voice still more.

"That's what everybody thinks, I hope," she said.

"Thinks?"

"Yes. The carters and the outriders are scattered around the bars, giving the impression they are spending the night in town, but they have their orders. Shortly after full dark the carts will roll, and being empty, they'll roll fast."

"Yes?" he prompted.

"Yes," she repeated. "So if anybody has a notion to stage a raid on the train tomorrow, they'll find themselves about a day late. I think my little stratagem will work, don't you?"

"Looks sort of that way," he conceded.

Personally, although he refrained from saying so, he was not as confident as he gave the impression of being. The success of the stratagem depended on nobody learning about it, and of late it appeared somebody was able to learn most anything. And a careless word dropped by a carter or outrider or other employee, with a wrong pair of ears listening, could nullify the scheme.

Also, it was readily apparent that the head of the owlhoot outfit operating in the section was inordinately shrewd and might well put two and two together and make four.

However, that somebody might meditate a raid on the money train was but presumption on his part, and there was nothing to be gained by causing the girl to needlessly worry; so he kept his misgivings to himself. Later he was to doubt the wisdom of his decision.

"Here comes Uncle John and the boys," Mary exclaimed. "I guess they're ready to get going."

They were, and called her to come along.

"Okay, dear," she said to Slade. "I'll see you tomorrow evening. Please take care of yourself."

She trotted out the door, smiling at him over her shoulder. Old John shouted an invitation to the Cross W ranchhouse when he could find the time.

Slade sat on in the Branding Pen for some time, smoking and thinking. He couldn't get that confounded cart train out of his mind. He told himself that his apprehensions were unfounded, but the feeling that something was going to happen to the train persisted. He went out and walked around for a while, watched the multi-colored glory of the sunset, went back to the Branding Pen for a cup of coffee and a snack, and set to thinking again.

Finally he gave up, and the result of his

irritating cogitations was the stable and the rig on Shadow's back.

"Going to play another of our loco hunches, horse," he told the big black. "Anyhow, there'll be a full moon and nice ambling. Okay?"

Shadow snorted derisively but appeared amenable to the suggestion, his powerful limbs hankering for action.

Now it was almost full dark. Slade rode out of the canyon in the shadow of the west wall and turned west on the trail. The moon had not yet risen and the night was quite gloomy, with a slight haze dimming the light of the stars.

A couple of miles out of Sanderson, the trail ran through a belt of not too dense thicket. Here Slade forced Shadow into the growth, rolled a cigarette and lounged comfortably in the saddle to wait.

He didn't have too long to wait. Less than an hour had passed when he heard the rumble of approaching wheels. A few minutes later the cart train hove into view and rolled past at a good pace, the outriders pretty well bunched, and the carters laughing and chatting together.

Slade shook his head in disapproval. Evidently the young fellows felt everything was as it should be, nothing to worry about. Which was not the proper attitude in this neck of the woods.

He waited until the train had gotten well ahead, then left his place of concealment and followed, keeping back far enough so that it was unlikely that he would be spotted, hugging the brush or the cliffs as he was, but close enough for his unusual eyes to take in every detail of the train and its surroundings.

Slade, who was familiar with every foot of the trail, knew that the likely spot for a try for the train, if one were made, was some miles farther on, almost halfway to Marathon, where low cliffs flanked the trail on the north, with thick brush encroaching on the south. And where a trail from the north joined the main track; a trail which circled around to the east, by way of which Sanderson could be reached. That was where the Marathon stage had been held up a couple of times in past years. So he rode on expectant, but not expecting anything to happen for some time.

Now the moon was well up in the sky, flooding the wild scene with silvery light, in which objects stood out hard and clear. Ahead and on and on, the mountains loomed closer; the Bullis Gap range, the Haymond Mountains, the higher peaks of the Pena Blanca Ranger, Woods Hollow Mountains, as yet unseen. And on the north the jagged mass of the Glass Mountains. On the left, sentinel of the Big Bend, Cathedral Mountain.

Walt Slade had heard someone call this region "The Land That God Forgot." It was not so. He had remembered, and remembered well. Slade thought here was one of the most sublime masterpieces of the Creator. Wild austere, rugged, grim; yes. But with an awesome beauty for those with eyes to see and understand.

Now the point was near where Slade believed the attempt, were one made, would take place; an ideal spot from the outlaw point of view. He closed the distance between him and the train quite a bit. Didn't matter much anymore if he was spotted by the carters. And now his gaze focused on the thick brush to the left, the low cliffs to the right.

Suddenly, on the crest of the cliff, only a few score yards ahead of where the cart train rolled, his keen eyes caught a flicker of light. He didn't know what it meant, except that it certainly boded no good for the train. His voice rang out,

"Trail, Shadow, trail!"

The great black lunged forward, almost instantly going at racing speed. Slade whipped his Winchester from the boot, dropped the knotted reins on Shadow's neck, and held the saddle gun ready for action, his eyes never leaving the cliff top.

A fluff of yellowish flame, a sullen boom! What in blazes were the devils trying to do, blow the cliff down to block the trail in front of the train? Lots of good that would do them!

They'd find themselves in the middle of a corpse-and-cartridge session for fair.

But echoing the boom of the explosion was a rending and splitting; then a muffled roar.

Over the shattered cliff edge gushed a torrent of water, flashing and scintillating in the moonlight. The downward-plummeting column struck squarely on the second from the lead cart.

Ensued confusion, compounded and complete. The terrified horses, the water foaming above their knees, plunged, reared, tried to turn. Over went a cart, and another; the drivers hurled through the air to strike the trail. An outrider's horse was knocked from its feet to add to the mad tangle.

And from the growth to the left bulged six masked horsemen, shooting as they came.

But now El Halcon was almost up to the rearmost cart. The Winchester spat flame. One of the horsemen whirled from the saddle as if struck by a pile driver on the loose. Another crackle from the big rifle and a second saddle was emptied. Answering bullets whined past, fanning his face, plucking at his shirt sleeve. He fired a third time, but the masked men, backing plunging, rearing horses, were on the far side of the falling column of water. The spray spoiled his aim and he scored a miss. He reeled slightly as a slug grazed his neck.

But the next shot made up for the miss. A third outlaw went down to lie motionless. The remaining three whirled their horses and fled west as the demoralized outriders, somewhat recovered, began blazing away. Slade fired a final shot before they careened around a bend a short distance ahead; he thought one lurched sideways but couldn't be sure in the deceptive moonlight.

To follow was out of the question. Shadow would need wings to get past the mad tangle in front. Besides, Slade was pretty sure somebody had been wounded by the raiders before he could get into action.

"Quiet the horses and get them under control!" he thundered above the tumult. "The waterfall's letting up and they'll be all right in a few moments."

He studied the cliff crest, but could see no sign of movement. Evidently the fellow who set off the explosion had discreetly hightailed. Now the falling water was not much more than a trickle.

"Mr. Slade!" suddenly howled one of the outriders. "Where did *you* come from?"

"Never mind," Slade replied. "Is anybody badly hurt?"

A brief survey of the situation relieved his anxiety. The carters who had been hurled from their seats were bruised and battered but already on their feet, cursing wholeheartedly. An outrider had a bullet-punctured shoulder, another a hole through the fleshy part of his arm. Those were the extent of the casualties, for which Slade was devoutly thankful.

"But if you hadn't showed up when you did,

right now we'd all be dead," a carter declared. "Those devils meant to murder us."

Slade didn't differ with him, feeling that he very likely had the right of it. Securing medicaments from his saddle pouch, he went to work on the wounded and quickly had them patched up.

"Will hold you till you see the doctor," he told them. The injuries were painful and both had lost considerable blood, but they were rugged young fellows and Slade did not anticipate any serious complications.

"Where in blazes did that blankety-blank water come from?" somebody wondered.

"There was evidently a pool up there," Slade explained. "Very likely rain water collected in a depression. A small charge of dynamite, properly set, blew a channel through the cliff lip. Fortunately nobody got hit by a chunk of falling rock. Well, it was a new wrinkle in owl-hoot operation; never heard of anything like it. Somebody has brains and knows how to use them."

"*Si*," quoth a Mexican carter, "but of the brains not enough is, to against El Halcon go."

Which provoked a general laugh, and general agreement. Slade smiled, and changed the subject.

"Suppose we take a look and see what we bagged," he suggested. "Got a lantern?"

A lantern was produced from one of the carts.

The masks were stripped from the dead outlaws' faces and everybody crowded around for a look. Nobody recalled seeing them before.

"Mean lookin' as striped snakes," was an outrider's verdict. The others nodded. Slade noticed nothing outstanding about them, although he felt their features, contorted though they were in the agony of death swift and sharp, indicated intelligence above that of the average cowhand, which their dress (and the marks of rope and branding iron on their hands, though faint), seemed to proclaim them to be—or to have been. None of them were young.

Their pockets produced a fairly large amount of money, which Slade passed to the head carter.

"Divide it up," he directed. "I figured you earned it, and the county treasury can do without it."

"How about you, Mr. Slade?" the carter asked. "You've earned it all, from my way of thinking."

Slade smiled, and shook his head with a finality that brooked no argument.

One pocket did divulge that which caused Slade's black brows to draw together thoughtfully; two more railroad torpedoes. He stowed them in his own pocket.

"Well, all this happened in Brewster County, not Terrell," he said. "So we'll load the bodies into one of the carts and pack them to Marathon, where Sheriff Chet Traynor is very likely to be;

he is most of the time. I see the horses these devils rode didn't bolt after the rest but are nosing around up the trail a piece. Catch them and we'll take them along; should realize enough to pay for burying their former riders. Let's get those overturned carts on their wheels and repair the harness best we can."

Both chores were taken care of and the train rolled on. Slade inspected the wounded and decided his first estimate of the damage was correct. Really nothing to worry about.

Slade turned in his saddle to gaze thoughtfully at the cliff top with its splintered tip. Not far ahead, he knew, was the north fork of the trail, by way of which Sanderson could be reached.

The delay had been quite prolonged and the sun was well up in the sky when they finally reached Marathon.

12

There was excitement aplenty when the carts stopped at Sheriff Traynor's Marathon office and their grisly burden was unloaded. Traynor himself came hurrying out, demanding particulars.

The carters and the outriders supplied them, and Slade's stock didn't fall any in the course of the telling.

"Somewhat over-colored but fairly accurate," he replied to the sheriff's inquiring glance. "We'll talk later. Right now I wish to finish with this carting business."

He nodded to the head carter, who hauled the money poke from beneath the feed sacks in the front cart. The purveyor of goods was located, his price paid, the carts loaded.

The doctor had been summoned. He examined Slade's handiwork with approval, changed the pads and bandages and told the sufferers,

"Go to bed or go get drunk, whichever you prefer."

The pair hurried off together, and there was little doubt as to their preference.

The bodies were laid out on the floor in the sheriff's office and were looked over by various citizens who could not recall seeing them before.

"Guess those two riders were darn lucky to get

nothing worse than nicks," Traynor remarked.

"Yes, if the light had been better and that waterfall kicking up less spray, they would probably not be here in shape to navigate," the Ranger conceded.

"And I gather if it hadn't been for you, none of the galoots would be here," Traynor remarked.

"Possibly," Slade admitted. "It's a killer bunch."

Finally the crowd dispersed. Traynor closed and locked the door.

"How in blazes did you catch on to what was going to happen?" he asked.

"I didn't," El Halcon answered. "I just played a hunch that the outlaw bunch had caught on to what was planned and aimed to take advantage of what appeared a nice opportunity. Hunch sort of paid off."

"They usually do," grunted the sheriff; "that is, where you are concerned. Sounds more to me like straight thinking. Anything else to add?"

"There's something I wish there was," the Ranger said thoughtfully.

"Yes?"

"Yes. I can't help but wonder if the fellow who set off the blast on the cliff top was the head man of the pack. The way it was handled evinced more than a little knowledge of explosives. The charge had just the right power. Otherwise it would have blown the cliff face to smithereens. The timing was perfect, the very short fuse cut to exactly the right length. The whole bizarre affair was original and unique, manifesting as it did the most careful planning and a meticulous attention to detail by one thoroughly familiar with the Sanderson-Marathon trail and its environs. I'm pretty well acquainted with the trail myself, but I didn't know that pool was up there."

"A darn shrewd customer, all right," Traynor agreed.

"Outlaw procedure usually runs to a pattern," Slade said. "So one has a chance to anticipate the moves. But the gentleman operating in the section at present does not conform to the accepted format. He goes off at a tangent in a most unexpected manner."

"Something to make even El Halcon stir his stumps, eh?" the sheriff chuckled. "Well, I know what the final outcome will be, so I ain't worryin'. Now what?"

"Now I can do with a bite to eat and a few hours of sleep while my horse is resting," Slade replied. "Suppose you'll hold some sort of an inquest?"

"Yep, we'll hold one, right here," said Traynor. "No sense in it, but the law's the law and I reckon we'd better conform, in a fashion. Guess we can round up enough of your boys from the various bars to act as witnesses."

"Expect you can," Slade agreed. "The carts won't start on the return trip until tomorrow morning. I'll head for Sanderson about sundown; be cooler riding at night."

"And keep your eyes skun," the sheriff advised. "The sidewinders might be out to try and even the score."

"Don't think they'll show much activity just yet, after what happened last night," Slade replied carelessly.

"Let's go eat," said Traynor. "I ain't had any breakfast yet, either. Place across the street all right, where you've eaten before?"

"Be fine," Slade answered. "Perhaps I can tie onto a room upstairs, as I did last time."

"You can," said the sheriff.

Shadow was placed in a stable the sheriff patronized, where Slade knew he would get the best of care. After eating, he slept in a comfortable bed until the late afternoon.

An impromptu inquest was held, the expected verdict arrived at. Slade said goodbye to Sheriff Traynor and headed for Sanderson in the red-gold glow of the sunset.

"Well, things didn't work out too bad," he told the horse. "But it was touch and go. If I'd miscalculated just a little, Mary would be short a poke of money, to say nothing of a number of her hands. All's well that ends well, as the saying goes, so june along, feller, we have fifty miles to cover."

"What's fifty miles!" Shadow's answering snort seemed to say as he lengthened his stride.

Slade enjoyed the ride through the moon-drenched beauty of the wastelands and wouldn't have cared if it had been prolonged. But Shadow, sensing oats in the offing, kept up his steady gait.

In the wee small hours of the morning they reached Sanderson. Slade cared for his mount and then made his way to the Branding Pen where, as he expected, he found Mary and Sheriff Crane anxiously awaiting him.

In reply to their questions, he gave a terse account of the affair on the Marathon trail. The sheriff swore under his mustache, the girl shuddered.

"And you saved my boys," she said. "Seems you always do the right thing at the right time. But how in the world did those terrible men learn what they did? It was supposed to be a dead secret."

"It is difficult to keep such a thing secret," Slade told her. "A careless word dropped in the wrong place could give the whole plan away. Suppose you drew the money from the bank?"

"Yes, I did," she admitted.

"That may have been noted," Slade said. "And the destination of the carts learned. Somebody hereabouts appears to have a genius for learning things. Anyhow, the trap was set."

"And were it not for you, it would have succeeded," Mary said.

"Possibly," Slade conceded. "Well, how about calling it a night? Soon be daylight."

The following afternoon, obeying an impulse, Slade dropped in at the Big Enough. He found Blaine Foster sitting at a table, writing a letter. Before him was an envelope and a signed check. He waved Slade to the opposite chair, beckoned a waiter to bring a drink.

"Sit down," he said. "Be through here in a few minutes. I'm writing a letter to my father. You see, Dad is pretty well-heeled and loaned me the money to buy and refurnish the Big Enough. If I'd failed up in the business, he would never have said a word about the loan, but he says when I'm doing all right, an obligation should be met as agreed on. No matter what it is or to whom. He brought up all us boys to feel that way."

"He's absolutely right," Slade interpolated.

"That's the way I feel about it," Foster said. "So each month I send him a check in payment on the advance. Be right with you."

His pen scratched busily for a few minutes. Then he folded the letter, slipped it and the check into the envelope, scrawled an address and affixed a stamp.

"There, that takes care of that," he announced. "Now we can talk. How's everything with you?"

"No cause for complaint," Slade replied. "And yourself?"

"Guess I've no right to complain, either," Foster said. "Except for a slight case of the itch," he added with a boyish grin.

"Itch!"

"Uh-huh. As I told you the other night, I got into the liquor business because there's money to be made in it, quick money. But, as I also told you, I was brought up on a spread and I guess I've still got hair rope and saddle leather in my blood. That's where the itch comes in; an itch to own a little spread and sorta get mixed up in the cow business. Guess you know old Jason Quimby who owns a small spread over to the west, the Four J? Well, Quimby is in the notion to sell out and move over east where what folks he's got left live. I've been dickering with him, and night before last we just about closed the deal. Do you think I'm being foolish; spreading myself too thin?"

"No, I don't," Slade answered. "It is good to have an occupation or a business that affords one pleasure. And in my opinion the cattle business is due for a boom before long; all the signs point that way."

"I'm sure glad to hear you say it," Foster declared gratefully. "I was just wondering a little. But if you approve, I know I'm doing the right thing. Waiter!"

Both smiling, they drank a toast to the venture.

Slade left the Big Enough in an equable frame

of mind. He chuckled more than once on his way to the sheriff's office and seemed highly amused at some prospect.

Crane fetched coffee from the back room, filled his pipe, and remarked casually,

"Moseyed into the Big Enough night before last. Foster wasn't around. Barkeep said he was out riding."

"As he had a perfect right to be, if he so desired," Slade replied.

"Guess maybe he figured it was a good night for a ride—at first," the sheriff said significantly.

"It was a beautiful night for a ride," Slade said. "A full moon and very still. I would have enjoyed a like peaceful amble."

"So you figure it was just a nice peaceful amble he was on, eh?"

"I do," Slade answered.

The sheriff stared at him and exclaimed peevishly, "I'm almost beginning to think you don't believe there is anything off-color about that hellion."

"States the case precisely," Slade said, smiling broadly.

"That's right," Slade said. "You can write Foster off, minus the 'color.' "

The sheriff said several things, none of them nice. "Then who the blankety-blank blue blazes have we got to suspect?" he concluded.

Slade ceased smiling. "That remains to be

learned, for sure, and proven," he answered soberly.

Crane asked a point-blank question,

"Have you a notion as to who he is?"

"The haziest of notions," Slade replied. "So hazy, in fact, that I wouldn't presume to mention it. I imagine Mary would call it intuition. Which, in a way, it is."

The sheriff gave vent to a hollow groan and declared, "Well, if the blankety-blank has tumbled to the fact that you are onto him, and has the brains you give him credit for having, right now he's like a snake looking at its tail—he sees his finish!"

Slade laughed heartily. "I fear the hypothetical gentleman in question would hold a different opinion," he said.

"Maybe," admitted the sheriff. "But I figure before long he'll be due to change his opinion. Finish your coffee and let's go eat. Expect your gal is waiting for us."

She was, with a slight case of the jitters.

"I've been sitting here chewing my nails and waiting for the carts to show," she confessed. "Walt, do you feel sure they'll be all right?"

"Don't worry, they will be," Slade reassured her. "The boys will be very much on the alert, and loaded for bear. Besides, the outlaws could hope for nothing from raiding the loaded carts. They'll be showing any minute now."

"I hope so," she sighed. "I'd hate for something else to happen to the boys. What happened night before last was bad enough."

"Not much more than scratches, they'll be healed up in a few days," he predicted cheerfully. "Both of them are tough as pine knots. I'll wager neither ever had a sick day in his life."

Slade proved to be a pretty good prophet. Before their orders were filled, the carting bunch streamed in, two boasting arm slings but chipper as the others.

Mary ran to them with solicitous inquiries, calling them by name, and a royal jabber ensued as they gave their version of the affair on the trail, considerably more vivid than Slade's, especially the part he played.

"Now we really have the straight of it," she said. "Give them all drinks, Mr. Hogan, as many as they desire."

Hardrock grinned and bobbed, and obeyed orders.

"Now I can really enjoy my dinner," she said, and proceeded to do so, Slade and the sheriff emulating her example. After a final cup of coffee, she said,

"I'm going over to my room to freshen up a bit. I was so bothered about the carts that I did a very sketchy job when I got up. No wonder Walt is paying more attention to the dance floor girls than he is to me. Maybe we can visit the

Big Enough and that nice Mr. Foster again."

"What do you think of Foster?" Slade asked casually, slanting an amused glance at the sheriff.

"I like him," Mary replied. "I think he is a sincere, ambitious man who should do well."

Crane rolled his eyes to the heavens but did not otherwise comment.

"Be seeing you," Mary said, and scampered out.

"And there goes feminine intuition!" the sheriff groaned. "Going right along with what you figure. How in blazes do you do it!"

In reply, Slade recounted his experience with the letter-writing, check-mailing Foster.

"So that explains how he got the money we were wondering about," Crane said.

"Yes," Slade agreed, "but there is one thing that is not explained; why did that hellion try to kill him? It bothers me, for Foster. Another try to murder him may be made."

"Figure Foster might know why?"

"If he does," Slade said, "for some unexplained reason he's not talking about it. Of course in such a matter there is sometimes a personal angle a man is reluctant to discuss with others. Foster may have made an enemy who holds a grudge. We agree that he is salty and quick-tempered. But somehow I don't go along with that explanation; I think it is something deeper. And if Foster does know who was back of the attempt against him, he's a better actor than I've given him credit for being. Well, I imagine we'll learn the truth, sooner or later."

"Yep, you'll learn it, if there's anything to be learned," said the sheriff. "Let us drink!"

Mary rejoined them after a while. "Now I feel better," she said. "And I'm sure I look better."

"You look wonderful under any circumstances," Slade told her.

The sheriff chuckled and twinkled his eyes at her. Mary wrinkled her nose at *him*.

13

They spent a pleasant and peaceful night at the Branding Pen and the Big Enough. Slade banished his problems from his mind and relaxed comfortably. To heck with them for the present.

As they walked slowly up Railroad Street, the sheriff glanced at the heavily overcast sky.

"Looks like it's going to rain," he observed.

It did, before dawn; a drencher which continued through most of the day. Toward evening the sky cleared. Slade, strolling about the town, gazed at the water tumbling from the cliff tops and rushing down the canyon.

"Someday," he predicted to a friendly lamppost, "there will be a real cloudburst hereabouts and this pueblo will stand a good chance of being washed off the map."

He gazed at the swirling water for another moment; then continued his stroll until he reached the sheriff's office.

"By the way," he said as he sat down, "here are a couple more railroad torpedoes you can stow with the other two. I took them off one of those fellows who tried to raid the cart train."

"Wonder why those devils are packing 'em around?" said Crane, dropping them in the drawer.

"I don't know," Slade replied, "but I've an uneasy feeling that it bodes no good."

He was definitely right.

The El Paso Flyer did not stop at Langtry but rolled on toward Sanderson. Exhaust booming, side rods clanking, the long string of coaches rocking and swaying behind it, the great locomotive roared on.

About twenty miles east of the division town, the track made a long, sweeping curve where thick chaparral encroached in both sides of the right-of-way. The engineer slowed his train a bit in deference to the curve.

Suddenly from the rails under the spinning drivers sounded the sharp snap-snap of torpedoes. The engineer obeyed the caution signal, shutting his throttle, gently applying the air to grind the brake shoes against the tires. The plume of smoke rising from the stack flattened out, rose again as the fireman twirled the blower valve. Both hogger and tallowpot leaned out their windows, gazing ahead.

Again that ominous "snap-snap." The engineer applied more air, the speed reduced to a crawl around the curve.

A little distance to the front a man in overalls and jumper, apparently a track walker, was waving a red flag back and forth across the track. That meant "stop!" The engineer opened the air brake valve wide. The train jolted to a standstill.

The man with the flag sauntered forward, glancing now and then at the growth on his left.

"What is it?" the engineer called.

"Washout, right around the curve," the other called back laconically.

The engineer nodded; it was not surprising, after the heavy downpour. Had happened more than once in the past.

The conductor was dropping from the steps of the rear coach. Heads were poking out windows. The express messenger opened the door of the express car and leaned out. The "track walker" now almost opposite the locomotive, waved his flag as if in a summoning gesture.

From the chaparral bulged six masked men, racing toward the stalled train. The express messenger tried to close his door, but the man in the lead of the bunch, tall, broad-shouldered, shot him before he could do so. He fell backward to the floor to lie motionless. The other raiders were taking pot shots at the coaches, where out-thrust heads had vanished as if by magic. The conductor dived back up the steps. The engineer and fireman crouched low in their cab, praying they wouldn't be noticed.

The tall man and another climbed into the express car, callously kicking the messenger's body aside. They sped across the car to where the safe stood open; the messenger, with Sanderson only a few minutes away, had been checking his accounts.

In a matter of minutes the safe was rifled of its contents; a very large sum of money, plus some valuable jewelry, which was transferred to a sack the tall man carried. Outside, their companions were still shooting at the coaches.

The pair turned, hurried back across the car and leaped to the ground.

Firing a final volley, the outlaws dashed into the brush, the pseudo track walker accompanying them. Another moment and fast hoofs sounded, fading northward.

The raging train crew rushed to the express car, but there was nothing to be done for the unfortunate messenger; he had been drilled dead center.

Curious passengers, who had disembarked, were hustled back into the coaches, the doors slammed shut.

Fearful of a possible obstruction on the track, the engineer eased his train very slowly around the curve. Then, with the straight-away clear before him, he proceeded to shatter a few speed records on the way to Sanderson.

When the Flyer screeched to a stop at the station, very quickly a bedlam-type uproar was in full swing. Railroad police from the yards swarmed over the train, asking questions nobody could answer.

The sheriff was sent for. He and Slade took their time reaching the station, for they knew very well there was nothing they could do there. Slade questioned the engineer and fireman as to the appearance of the man who posed as a track walker, but both admitted they didn't get anything like a good look at his face; hat pulled low, a neckerchief muffled high.

The messenger's body was removed to the sheriff's office. The Flyer, with a crew change and a fresh engine, finally got under way, more than an hour late.

"Well, the devils put one over," Crane remarked as he and the Ranger returned to the office.

"Yes, they did, very neatly," Slade said. "Now we know, just a trifle late, why they were packing railroad torpedoes."

"If we'd guessed, I don't see as there would have bccn anything we could do about it," replied Crane. "We could hardly have patrolled the whole blasted railroad."

"Yes, that's so," Slade admitted. "It was a very smoothly handled move. Nothing particularly new about it; has been done before. I recall one on the Mexican National Railways south of Juarez across from El Paso. Was very much the same."

"Seven of the devils today," remarked the sheriff. "And you've already done for more than seven. Ain't there no end to them!"

"It is, or was, a big bunch," Slade said. "Of course they may be getting recruits to replace losses. I'm convinced it is not a Texas band. Arizona or New Mexico, I'd say. Several big Arizona outfits were smashed and scattered by the Arizona Rangers under Captain Ross, and such sheriffs as John Slaughter. Many of them went to California, but it's logical to believe some drifted this way. Well, they're well-heeled for a while now. There was a lot of money in that express car safe, and, I understand, quite a bit of high-priced jewelry."

"Maybe they'll try to dispose of that and give us a line on 'em," hoped Crane.

"They'll dispose of it, all right, but not around here," Slade replied. "The head of the outfit is too smart and experienced to try that."

"Guess so," agreed the sheriff. "That poor devil of a messenger never had a chance."

"It's a killer bunch," Slade said. "I feared somebody would be killed in the course of their next raid. Well, it happened. And it'll happen again unless we are able to prevent it by anticipating what their move will be. That's becoming monotonous in the line of hopeful thinking."

"You didn't do so bad figuring in advance the raid on the cart train," Crane pointed out.

"As I told you, that was in the nature of following a hunch," Slade smiled.

"Okay, just keep on following them and

everything will be hunky-dory," said the sheriff. "Well, about time to put on the nosebag. When's Mary going back to the spread?"

"Tomorrow," Slade replied. "And I think I'll ride with her. Old John planned to come in yesterday or today, but didn't feel up to the ride, Echols said. I'll be back day after tomorrow. Try and keep out of trouble for that long."

"You should talk!" snorted Crane. "It just nacherly follows you around."

14

A little before noon the following day, Slade and Mary did ride north, in bright and balmy weather.

"The rangeland is always at its best after a rain," the girl remarked. "Look at the Texas bluebells peeping through the grass. They're holding their little cups up to the sun, to offer thanks."

As they passed through Echo Canyon, Slade said,

"After I tuck you away safe in the casa, I think I'll ride on up to the Rocking L. I want to see how Griswold Hale is making out with his artesian well project."

"Please let me go with you," Mary instantly begged. "I'd love to."

"Okay, if that's the way you feel about it," he acceded.

"And I know a short-cut to the Rocking L, across the range," she added. "We'll bypass our casa and save miles of riding."

Slade didn't argue, for she knew the section as she knew the palm of her hand. He recalled the first time they had met, when her extensive knowledge had saved them from disaster.

They rode steadily and reached the Rocking L ranchhouse something after the middle of the afternoon. Hale was sitting on the front porch when they rode up. He had a hearty greeting for both.

"How's your drilling coming along?" Slade asked.

"Just fine," Hale replied. "Already brought in one well. It's artesian, all right, as you said it would be. Like to ride over for a look?"

"We'd be greatly pleased to," Slade assured him.

"Okay, I'll have the rig put on my cayuse," Hale said. "After we come back, we'll have a snack."

First they visited the well that had come in. Here a column of silvery water was shooting ten feet into the air. Already a little stream was flowing west across the range. Nearby a large shallow waterhole was being dug, which would be filled from the stream.

"Not bad," Halc said.

"Very good," was Slade's comment.

They rode on for a mile or more, to where the drilling rig was chugging away blithely, the steel bit biting into the earth. They pulled up at a little distance. Hale watched the operation a moment,

"Excuse me," he said. Dismounting, he approached the rig, said a few words to the operator. The man nodded, and made a slight adjustment.

"He is thoroughly conversant with drilling," Slade murmured to Mary. "Only an expert would have noted that slight deviation which was causing the rope to chafe in the pulley."

The girl gave him a quick glance but did not comment.

Hale returned and forked his saddle.

"Now back to the ranchhouse for coffee and a bite," he said.

The snack set before them was bountiful and they did full justice to it. Hale proved an affable host.

"Please come again," he begged, as they prepared to ride for the Cross W ranchhouse. "Expect I'll drop in on your uncle in the next day or two, Miss Mary."

"Well?" Slade asked as they rode south.

"He is charming when he wishes to be, and a perfect gentleman so far as manners are concerned, but I don't like him," Mary replied. "He *looks* at me."

"Well, you can't blame him for that," Slade chuckled.

"Oh, he doesn't look at me *that* way," she said. "I wouldn't mind if he did. Mr. Foster looks at me *that* way, and I feel complimented. So do you, my dear, at least sometimes. Mr. Hale's look is appraising, the sort of look that Uncle John bestows when he is trying to make up his mind about buying stock, as to whether or not it will be a good investment. That's the sort of look with which Mr. Hale favors me."

"Well, that's the penalty you must pay for being affluent," Slade smiled.

"Lots I care about affluence, and you know it," she retorted. "I could do without every bit of it, for the right man. Remember the last stanza of one of the songs you wrote, my dear; THE GYPSY LOVER:—

> He took me from my silks and furs,
> My gold and jewels spurning.
> My feet are bare, my gown's a rag,
> Heighho! I'm not returning!

"That's little Mary, my dear, as you very well know."

Slade laughed heartily, but almost immediately, the concentration furrow was deep between his black brows. A sure sign, as she well knew, that El Halcon was doing some concentrated thinking.

Slade gazed back the way they had come. The Rocking L range, he knew, was long, east by west, but narrow, north by south. On the north it ran into the rugged hills for some distance. It was not considered a very good spread and Hale had doubtless gotten it for a small outlay. However, an ample water supply would enhance its value.

Without incident, they reached the ranchhouse to find old John quite chipper.

"That big rainstorm on the way had me down," he said. "Fall weather in the offing that way affects old bones, but now I feel fine. See you got him home safe, chick, without any trouble."

"Yes," agreed Mary. "He should have me along all the time. Well, thank goodness, he wasn't mixed up in that affair on the railroad; he would have charged the lot of them."

"He'd have made out," Webb said cheerfully.

"Probably have accomplished a fine but futile end after knocking off a few outlaws," Mary returned.

"It would have been the outlaws that made a what-you-call-it end," Webb insisted. "End over end with bad cases of lead pizening. Don't worry about him."

After spending a pleasant evening and night at the Cross W casa, Slade set out for Sanderson in the early afternoon.

"I'll be in tomorrow, and so will a couple of the boys and Uncle John," Mary said as they parted. "He's dispensing with the sling and feels much better."

Some distance from the ranchhouse, Slade turned in the saddle and gazed north toward the Rocking L spread and the rugged hills beyond.

"Shadow," he said, as he faced to the front, "I believe it's tying up. Still a few loose ends banging around, but I'm sure now they will weave into the needed pattern. June along, horse, we have things to do."

Slade rode warily, but reached Sanderson

without anything untoward happening. After caring for his horse, and having a chat with Sheriff Crane, he dropped in at the Big Enough, where Foster greeted him warmly.

"Been away?" the owner asked. "Missed you last night."

In reply, Slade mentioned his visit to the Rocking L and commented on the artesian well project. Foster listened in silence and sat gazing out the window at the sunset glow, his eyes brooding. Abruptly he seemed to reach a decision. He turned to the Ranger and said,

"Mr. Slade, I'm going to tell you something. I hope you won't spread it around. Somehow, I feel it is something you should know."

"Yes?" Slade prompted, his curiosity aroused.

"Yes," Foster repeated. "Mr. Slade, I recall Griswold Hale from Arizona; I saw him in Tombstone and Galeyville. That was some years ago and I was quite young, but I remember him. He associated with the Curly Bill Brocius bunch, of whom of course you have heard. He went around with Ringo, Hill, and the Clantons; was, without doubt, one of the bunch, so you can draw your own conclusions. I haven't mentioned it to a soul here, and I don't intend to. Far be it from me to put anything in the way of a man who has changed his early habits and is going straight, as it appears Hale is. But as I said, I just feel you should know about it."

Walt Slade regarded him with compassionate eyes, and with respect, and with a feeling of regret.

"Thank you, Foster, for telling me," he said. "And," he added cryptically, "you can rest assured that neither would I put anything in the way of a man who is trying to go straight."

To himself he mused exultantly, "And now I know why the attempt to murder Foster was made. Tying up, tying up fast!"

"Brocius was an unusual man, and attracted a varied lot," Foster resumed reminiscently. "There was Ringo, splendid brave, a gentleman in every sense of the word, but constantly brooding over past wrongs, finally a suicide. Hill, which was not his real name, the black sheep member of a respectable Arizona family. Billy Clanton, wild, reckless, but of intense loyalty and indomitable courage. And others who were just plain rapscallions of the worst kind. And I feel safe in saying that Griswold Hale was in the beginning of good family, and a man of ability."

"Yes, he is that," Slade agreed soberly.

Slade knew that the Brocius outfit was the largest, best-organized and most efficient criminal band the Southwest ever knew. Utterly ruthless, men, without mercy.

"I once heard in a roundabout way," Foster concluded, "that when Hale first came to Arizona he was employed by one of the Tucson copper mines in an engineering capacity, or something of the sort, and was discharged for something he insisted he was not guilty of. That may have been what turned him onto the wrong track."

"Not impossible," Slade conceded.

After promising Foster he and Mary would drop in the following night, he left the Big Enough and strolled about town, pondering what he had learned. Finally he turned his steps to the sheriff's office, where he regaled Crane with an account of Foster's dissertation on Griswold Hale and his former associates. The sheriff stared at him wide-eyed.

"For the love of Pete!" he exploded. "Betcha you've had your eye on that hellion right from the beginning."

"I'll admit I've been curious about him ever since Mary and I met him on the trail," Slade replied.

"Why?"

"Because he lied."

"Lied?"

"Yes, when he said he knew little about drilling and artesian wells. I knew he lied; that to the contrary his knowledge was exhaustive. Only a person pretty well grounded in geological phenomena would have recognized the possibilities of the trough between the two ranges of hills. And when a man lies to me, for no apparent reason, I become interested in him.

"Then when that attempt was made to drygulch me, a little later the same day, not so very long after we met Hale, I became a little more interested.

"I think that Hale, smart as he is, miscalculated a little, figuring I would be riding back to town later in the evening. Anyhow, he set his trap. He is thorough, and very likely another drygulcher was watching the canyon trail against the chance I'd follow that route.

"Of course, linking Hale with the attempted drygulching was largely surmise on my part, but what happened seemed to me just a little too pat to attribute to coincidence. Nobody knew my plans when Mary and I rode with the sheriff to fetch in the bodies of the devils who tried to kill Joyce Echols, and it was logical to assume we would ride back with the sheriff to attend the inquest. So, to all appearances, Hale was the only person who knew that instead we continued to the Cross W ranchhouse. See?"

"Yes, I see, after you put it before me," the sheriff answered wearily. "What else?"

"Several little things we'll go into later," Slade replied. "Like his always being around just before something was pulled, like the try for the carts, evincing engineering knowledge, and his appearance tallying pretty well with that of the leader of the outlaw bunch, big, tall, well set up. And Mary's instinctive dislike for him, which I didn't discount. Incidentally, Foster's appearance tallied pretty well, too. But what really convinced me, in my own mind, that Hale was the real outlaw leader, was his voice."

"His voice?"

"Yes. You'll recall that the night before I arrived here, I slept in a thicket close to a pool of water beside the trail. That riders paused there to let their horses tie onto a drink. And you'll remember, of course, that I heard one speak, giving orders relative to the fire that was used as a cover-up for the attempted station robbery. His voice was a cultured voice, nicely modulated. Well, when I heard Hale speak, the similarity of the two voices was startling. So much so that there was no doubt in my mind but that Hale was our man. Foster also has a nice voice, but different.

"Of course where Hale clinched the case against himself, although we didn't realize it at the time, was the attempt to kill Foster. Now we know the motive. Just as Foster recognized him, Hale recognized Foster and knew he was aware of Hale's former association with the Brocius gang. Hale evidently feared Foster would spread the word around and determined to get rid of him as quickly as possible. Perhaps he did not realize that Foster had already spotted him and aimed to do Foster in before he did. And very nearly succeeded."

“And if it wasn’t for you, he would have succeeded,” the sheriff interpolated.

“And so there you are;” Slade concluded, “the grand jury voting no bill. Surmise, speculation, guess work, with no foundation of fact; definitely non-proven.”

“Same old story!” snorted Crane. “Got to get the hellion dead to rights, or plumb dead.”

“Looks that way,” Slade conceded. “Little doubt but we are up against members of the old Brocius outfit, and they’re smart and bad. Another item; you doubtless recall that none of those we have managed to bring in were young. Which would tend to link them with Brocius so far as the time element is concerned.”

“And grabbin’ off the devils is going to be a chore,” Crane said.

“If past performance is any criterion, it certainly is,” Slade agreed. “Well, we’ll see.”

“It’ll work out,” the sheriff predicted cheerfully. “Well, guess a little coffee is in order, to help us think.”

The coffee was procured and for some time they sat sipping and smoking.

“Wonder if Hale intends to eventually go straight?” Crane suddenly remarked. “The way he is fixing up the spread he bought looks a mite that way.”

“Barely possible,” Slade replied. “But experience leans to the contrary. The lure of easy money, so called, is usually too strong for such men to resist. The express car robbery netted the bunch more than the cost of the ranch and the improvements. The ranch is an excellent cover-up, and enables him, as a respectable cattleman, to learn things. Somehow, he managed to find out the Flyer was packing much more money than it ordinarily does. The same applied to the Fenwick store raid."

"Guess that's so," Crane agreed. "He's a plumb smart hellion, all right. No doubt about that."

Another period of silence ensued, then the sheriff asked,

"Think he has any notion you're a Ranger?"

"I would say no," Slade answered. "I believe he goes for the El Halcon yarn. I do think, however, that he gives me credit for having some knowledge of the principles of engineering. Foster heard it straight when he was told Hale had been employed by the copper mines interests. I'm confident he is a mining engineer. The way he handled that chore of turning the water onto the cart train would convince me of that, even had there been no other indications. Yes, a shrewd, competent man with his talents turned into the wrong channels. A pity. But there are so many of them, and they pose the law enforcement officer the worst problem."

"You've gone up against that sort before and always came out on top," Crane reminded him.

"As I've said before, my money's on El Halcon, who not only outshoots them but outthinks them as well."

Slade laughed. "So far," he said, "I'd say I've just had the better luck when it came to shooting. I can't help but feel the rapscallion is always a jump ahead of me."

"He'll jump short, sooner or later," the sheriff predicted blithely. "Well, how about the Branding Pen and a surrounding? All this gabbin' has got me lank."

Slade was agreeable and they headed for Hardrock's place, which they found going strong although the hour was still early. Hardrock came over to join them while they waited to be served.

"Your *amigo*, Mr. Hale, was in a little while ago," he announced. " 'Pears to be in a good humor. Had several of his hands with him, the old Rocking L bunch he kept on when he took over the holding. Bought 'em all a couple of drinks. Said if I saw you to tell you he struck pay dirt, another well came in."

"He struck pay dirt, all right, but he wasn't referring to artesian wells," Slade remarked after Hardrock had returned to the end of the bar. The sheriff growled and snorted.

"Hellion's laughing at us," he grumbled. "He'll laugh on the other side of his face before you're done with him. The ornery blankety-blank!"

Slade laughed and set to work on his meal.

After he finished eating and downed a snort, the sheriff announced his intention to return to his office where he had some paper work to take care of.

"Wonder why Hale came in tonight?" he remarked as he prepared to leave.

"I wish I knew," Slade replied. "I don't think he ever does anything without a reason. He may have something in mind; wouldn't be surprised if he has, and that we'll hear about it later, and not like the hearing."

Crane growled a cussword or two and stalked out. Slade sat on in the Branding Pen, thinking.

In answer to a sudden impulse, he left the Branding Pen and made his way to the Big Enough. Foster was not in evidence.

"Rode off just a little while ago," the bartender said. "Headed for the Four J over to the west, Jason Quimby's placc. Understand he and Quimby have a deal on. Packed a rather hefty passel of money with him. Guess he won't be back until late tomorrow."

Outside the Big Enough, Slade stood for a few minutes, deep in thought. Abruptly he headed for Shadow's stable at a fast pace.

"Going to play another loco hunch," he told the horse as he cinched up. "If it happens to be a straight one and we don't do something about it, tonight a man is going to die. Let's go!"

15

After leaving Sanderson, Slade rode with loose rein, allowing Shadow to gradually build up speed. The trail to the Four J ran for miles over the open prairie softly aglow with the starshine. Not until the Four J ranchhouse was but a comparatively short distance ahead did it turn into broken ground of ridges, gulleys and ravines.

With only the stars in the sky, visibility was fairly good. Later there would be a moon, which would help. Slade did not think an attempt would be made against Foster on the open rangeland. But the broken land beyond would be ideal for a drygulching.

So he felt it was up to him to overtake the Big Enough owner before he reached that ominous terrain. Constantly he scanned the far reaches in hope of catching sight of his quarry. But the rangeland lay lonely and deserted save for clumps of feeding cattle. And as the miles flowed back, he became increasingly anxious. Finally his voice rang out—"Trail, Shadow, trail!"

With a joyous snort, the great horse lunged forward, and within a matter of seconds was fairly racing across the prairie, his rider's eyes fixed on the shadowy northwest.

The moon rose and the rangeland glittered

with silvery light; it was almost as bright as day.

But still the far-flung grasslands lay untenanted. Slade's anxiety increased.

And then his amazing eyes found what they sought; a mere bouncing blob that quickly took form and shape, resolved into a single horseman riding at a fair pace.

Slade drew a breath of relief. Undoubtedly it was Foster, and still quite a way from the broken ground; Shadow would overtake him before he reached it. Slade settled himself more comfortably in the hull, his mind at ease. With him accompanying the Big Enough owner, there was little to fear from an attempted ambush.

And then abruptly the situation changed drastically, and for the worse.

From behind a clump of thicket to the northeast bulged seven horsemen, diagonalling toward where Foster rode.

Slade muttered an angry oath, but admitted a grudging admiration. Hale, the cunning devil, realized that with odds of seven to one, it would be easier and safer to ride down the lone horseman and kill him on the moon-bright prairie than to risk a drygulching in the gloom of the broken ground. And he had a good chance to do just that.

Blaine Foster was no fool, and he was a plainsman. Slade saw his head turn to study the advancing group. He altered his course more to the west. The bunch also altered a bit. Foster altered still more. The pursuers did likewise. From their ranks spurted fire. A moment later Slade heard the clang of the report. Foster hunched low in the saddle. And the race with death was on.

Another spurt of fire, another report. There was scant chance of scoring a hit at that distance; the devils were just serving notice of their intention. A sort of cat-and-mouse game of cruelty.

Foster was getting all he could from his horse, but the pursuers were gaining, though slowly. And El Halcon was still far away. He estimated the distance that separated him from the outlaws. Too great; nearly twelve hundred yards. He spoke urgently to Shadow, who managed to slightly increase his already flying gait.

The twelve hundred shrank to a thousand. Still too much, with the outlaws steadily gaining on their intended victim. Looked like Foster was a goner.

But the devils would pay a price for his murder, El Halcon grimly resolved. On the open prairie and forking Shadow, he had little to fear from them, if Foster was downed. But closing in on them with him still in the saddle would be a different matter.

Nine hundred yards—eight hundred! The legs of the triangle of which Foster was the point were shortening, and the gallant black horse was straining every nerve.

Now the owlhoots had sighted him, for he could see the white blurs of their faces turning in his direction. Slade drew his Winchester from the boot. Seven hundred yards! He waited another moment. His voice rang out,

"Steady, Shadow, steady!"

Instantly the horse levelled off to a smooth-running walk that hardly jolted his rider. Slade flung the Winchester forward. The muzzle gushed flame. He saw heads duck.

"A mite high," he muttered. "Less wind than I thought." Again he squeezed the trigger.

This time there was no mistake; a man pitched from his saddle to lie motionless. The big rifle blasted again, and there were two riderless horses plunging across the plain.

But now the distance separating him from the outlaws was less than five hundred yards. Answering bullets whined past, close. Packing saddle guns this time, eh?

Foster had halted and was blazing away with his six. Distance too great for short-gun work.

A slug just grazed the top of Slade's left shoulder as he lined sights; jolted him with the shock. He recovered, flung the rifle forward. Again the thundering boom. Three down,

That was enough for the raiders. The remaining

four whirled their mounts and streaked for the sanctuary of the broken ground.

Slade tried to pick his target, but there were two tall men of about equal height, and as he made his choice, pure guesswork, and squeezed the trigger, a patch of cloud drifted across the face of the moon, dimming the light. He thought he saw the fellow lurch in the saddle but couldn't be sure. Anyhow, he kept his seat.

Another cloud patch, thicker, and the light went out like a snuffed candle. Slade disgustedly emptied the magazine in the general direction taken by the fleeing raiders, pulled the blowing Shadow to a halt and began reloading.

The cloud moved on. Light funneled down, and he saw Foster riding toward him.

"Mr. Slade!" he exclaimed as he drew near. "You did it again! I thought I was a dead duck. Are you always at just the right place at just the right time?"

Slade smiled, and neither affirmed nor denied as he finished his reloading and thrust the Winchester back in the boot.

"Let's see what the bag is," he suggested.

They rode to where the bodies lay, dismounted and examined them.

"Say!" Foster exclaimed over the second, "this fellow was in the Big Enough shortly before noon today, I'm sure."

"I'm not surprised to hear it," Slade said dryly.

Foster studied the third dead man for some moments, his brows knit.

"It seems to me I've seen this one before," he said slowly. "That purple birth mark on the side of his face sort of stirs a chord of memory."

"Perhaps in Arizona?" Slade suggested.

"Could be," Foster conceded. "I do feel that he was younger when I saw him."

Slade nodded. "Interesting," he commented.

"What are we going to do about them?" Foster asked.

"Leave them for the sheriff to pack in," Slade replied. "I wish him to see them just as they are." Foster nodded his understanding.

"Well, I guess I might as well ride on to the Four J and keep my appointment with Jason Quimby," he said. "I'm a mite shaky, but all right."

"You'll do nothing of the sort," Slade told him flatly. "If those four devils who escaped—one of whom I'm pretty sure is the head man of the pack—were to hole up and wait for us, we'd be settin' quail for fair. You're riding back to Sanderson with me."

"I never thought of that," Foster said. "Seems you think of everything."

"Not everything, I fear," Slade replied smilingly. "Here's a little advice I think you would do well to heed. The next time you plan to take a lonely ride at night, don't mention, to anybody, that you intend to pack along a large sum of money. People with the best of intentions sometimes talk out of turn when the wrong pair of ears are listening. Because you are packing that money is one of the reasons, perhaps the only one, that you were attacked tonight."

"Guess I was foolish," Foster admitted, "stowing it in the poke at the bar. I won't do it again."

"Well, the horses have gotten their wind back, so we might as well be moving," Slade said. "The nags those three rode bolted in the direction of town and perhaps we can round them up and remove the rigs so they'll be comfortable. Yes, there they are, standing beside a little stream about a mile ahead. Got over their scare, it would appear."

"I don't know what kind of eyes you've got," marveled Foster. "I can't see anything. No horses, not even the crick."

A little later, however, he did.

The horses offered no objection to having the rigs removed and appeared glad to be able to drink and graze in comfort. The chore taken care of, Slade and Foster rode on their way.

"Tomorrow," the Ranger said, "Sheriff Crane and his deputies will ride up with pack mules or a wagon to collect the bodies. I'll ride with him, and seeing as it isn't far from there, we'll escort you to the Four J ranchhouse and you can complete your deal with Quimby and ride back to town with us."

"That will be wonderful," Foster replied gratefully. "I'm getting scared of my own shadow."

"A good notion to stay scared a little," Slade said. "May enable you to live longer."

Without incident they reached Sanderson, well past midnight. After putting up their cayuses, they headed for the Branding Pen, where Slade was pretty sure Sheriff Crane would be waiting.

He was, and his comments on the story they had to tell smoked, and smelled of sulphur.

"Twice he's saved my bacon," Foster interpolated.

Slade regarded him for a moment, while the sheriff regarded Slade, expectantly, knowing he was arriving at a decision. Finally the Ranger said.

"Foster, I would say you have given assurance that you can keep a tight latigo on your jaw, so I'm going to tell you something which I think will be to your advantage to know; will at least enable you to keep a watch on a certain individual."

"Yes?" replied Foster, also looking expectant.

"Yes," Slade repeated. "The man who tried to have you murdered is the man you knew in Arizona, Griswold Hale."

Foster blinked and stared. "But—but for the love of Pete, why?"

"Because," Slade explained, "he has been

afraid you would reveal his association with the Brocius outfit. Perhaps he still is, of that I'm not sure. Tonight he may have been interested only in the money you were packing, but then again he may have seen an opportunity to knock off a couple of pigeons with the same rock. Anyhow, he intended to kill you."

"And were it not for you, he would have accomplished it," Foster declared emphatically.

"At least now you know whom to keep an eye on," Slade concluded.

"And I will," Foster promised. "Well, if you don't mind, I'm going to bed. Guess it's the letdown; I feel quite tuckered. See you in the morning."

With another word of thanks, he departed. Slade and the sheriff watched him go.

"What you told him may keep him from falling into some trap Hale might set for him," observed the latter.

"I hope so," Slade said. "His intentions were of the best, but he badly misjudged Hale when he thought he had resolved to go straight. Hale is the ruthless killer type, and there is no reforming that sort."

"Except with a good dose of lead pizening," growled Crane. "Well, guess we'd better knock off a little ear pounding if we aim to get an early start up there."

Slade agreed and they headed for bed.

16

Shortly after noon, the sheriff's posse and Foster rode to the scene of the gunfight. Accompanying them was a light wagon to accommodate the bodies.

"Feller who rents these things is getting rich," grumbled Crane, with a glance at the wagon. "Well, guess the money is spent for a good cause. Maybe we'll find enough in those horned toads' pockets to pay the bill," he added hopefully.

They did, and more besides. The horses, which had not strayed far from the creek, would also bring a good price.

As the bodies were loaded into the wagon, Slade remarked,

"The short, heavy-set one is the devil who tried to stick a knife in Foster's back. Well, he finally got what was coming to him."

"Yep," agreed Crane. "Those Winchester slugs make nice big holes."

A little later they pulled into the astonished Jason Quimby's ranchhouse yard. Explanations followed.

"Well," said Quimby, "I'm sure glad to be sellin' out and trailing my twine away from this blasted section; gets worse all the time."

“It will eventually quiet down,” Slade predicted.

“Uh-huh, it may at that, if you stick around,” Quimby said.

The various documents were signed and witnessed and ready for legal approval and registration. Quimby was paid his money which he requested the sheriff to deposit for him at the Sanderson bank.

“Well, you’re in the cow business again,” Slade observed to Foster.

“And I’m darn glad to be,” the other returned. “Mr. Quimby’s hands will stay on with me.”

“They ain’t as young as they used to be and not in the notion of traipsin’ off somewhere,” Quimby said. “Good luck to you, Blaine, I got a feeling you’ll need all you can tie onto.”

“I’ll make out,” Foster replied. “Especially with Mr. Slade riding herd on me.”

Quimby chuckled, and didn’t differ.

“Not a bad night’s work you did,” Crane remarked complacently to Slade as they started on the return trip to Sanderson. “Three more to chalk up for our side. I’ve a notion *amigo* Hale is getting short of hired hands, wouldn’t you say, Walt?”

“Yes, I think he has but three left,” Slade replied. “I doubt if any more came from the west, or will come. But four smart and desperate men can cause plenty of trouble.”

"It'll be taken care of," said the sheriff. "I figure his twine is getting mighty, mighty short."

"But still long enough to twirl a tight loop," Slade added his own metaphor.

Which seemed to amuse the sheriff.

The outlaws' horses, which had not strayed far from the water, were rounded up, the rigs dumped into the wagon to keep the bodies company. The equipage rolled on to town, arriving as dusk was falling.

There was the usual gathering of the curious at the sheriff's office; however, such occurrences had been so frequent of late that not as much excitement was created as might have been expected.

The bodies were laid out on the floor, Quimby's money locked in the sheriff's safe, the horses looked after. All hands sojourned to the Branding Pen for a much-needed surrounding.

There they found Mary Merril and John Webb awaiting them, demanding an account of the previous night's hectic activities.

Slade complied, tersely, omitting salient details. Whereupon Foster took up the story and electrified his hearers with a vivid narration.

"Took on all seven of the devils by himself, did for three, sent the others skalleyhootin'," he concluded.

"I'm glad you were there, Mr. Foster," Mary said. "Otherwise we would never have learned what really happened. Just luck and all the breaks, to hear him tell it."

"Mr. Foster must be complimented for an outstanding imagination," El Halcon replied. Which remark was received with jeers.

All in all, it was a gay party. Hardrock joined them. The cook outdid himself. A toast was drunk to the success of Foster's venture into the cattle business. Mary danced with him, and with Slade. The sheriff and old John exchanged reminiscences over snorts. The young deputies found the dance floor girls congenial, and receptive.

And across the star-burned prairie, four grim men rode the vengeance trail.

The following afternoon, Slade strolled about the town for a while. Everything seemed peaceful. He watched the sunset and as the dusk deepened, followed his usual path up Railroad Street. He paused at the Big Enough for a word with Foster.

"Yes, I'll bring Mary in later," he promised. "She wants to come. Be seeing you."

He continued on his way, walking slowly, and thinking. He had almost reached a corner when from around it came cries for help. He quickened his stride, turned the corner.

A few yards distant a man, yelling for help, was sprawled on the ground. Over him stood two men, apparently kicking and beating him.

Slade started forward, then went sideways and down in a lightning shift as he sensed movement in a dark doorway across the street.

A gun blazed, a bullet whizzed over his prostrate form. Prone on the ground, he drew and shot, and again.

From across the street came a gasping cry, and a thud. Slade whirled his guns around, but the "beaten" man and his assailants were in full flight down the street. They swerved around the next corner even as he snapped a shot at them, and kept going.

Across the street, a body lay half out of the doorway, motionless.

His Colts ready for instant action, Slade got to his feet, his gaze never leaving the still form. He glided across the street. A single close glance told him the fellow was dead.

Voices were sounding in the distance, drawing nearer. Slade slipped back around the corner to Railroad Street and continued on his way; he had no desire to be pestered by questions.

Reaching the sheriff's office, he sauntered in. Crane eyed him suspiciously as he poured coffee.

"Thought I heard some shootin' somewhere," he remarked significantly.

"Wouldn't be surprised," was the Ranger's composed answer. "Lots of shooting hereabouts of late."

The sheriff fumed under his mustache but asked no questions, at the moment.

A few minutes later, as they sipped their coffee, fast steps sounded outside. An excited man burst in.

"Sheriff!" he yelped. "Sheriff, there's a dead feller layin' down on Fourth Street, just around the corner from Railroad. Got two bullet holes in him."

"Then I reckon he'll keep," replied Crane. "Set down until I finish my coffee and I'll go along with you for a look."

The man did so, fidgeting. The sheriff took his time with the coffee, glowering at Slade, whose lips twitched in a grin.

Finally he shoved his empty cup aside. "All right," he told the informant, "let's go." Slade accompanied them.

When they reached the body, they found quite a crowd surrounding it, conjecturing, speculating.

"A mean-lookin' jigger, Sheriff," somebody volunteered.

"Plenty of mean-lookin' ones hereabouts," said Crane. "Well, meanness usually gets a feller into trouble, sooner or later. Pack him to my office and put him on the floor with the others. Getting quite a collection. Doc can hold an inquest on all of 'em tomorrow."

The chore of "packing" was taken care of.

Crane shooed the crowd out and shut and locked the door.

"Okay, let's hear it," he said to Slade, who obliged.

"A very neat try," the Ranger concluded. "It might have worked if the drygulcher holed up across the street hadn't stepped forward a little as he lined sights. That was a mistake."

"A darn bad one for him," the sheriff interpolated dryly. "Go ahead."

"Yes, it was neat," Slade repeated. "Smarter than leaving a 'dead' man on the ground to distract the intended victim's attention, which has been done. Evidently when the other three saw me go down, they figured he had gotten me and hightailed. Corner was close, so they got around it in time."

"Well, guess that cuts the number down to three, including Hale," the sheriff said.

"So I would presume," Slade agreed. "Which is still three too many."

"Right about that," Crane conceded. "But the way you're cuttin' 'em down, three won't last long. Let's go eat."

As they opened the door, they met Blaine Foster hurrying in, his expression anxious. His face cleared, however, when his eyes rested on Slade, and he drew a breath of relief.

"Heard somebody was shot and I worried," he explained.

"Don't worry about *him,*" the sheriff replied, pointing to the body.

"Good heavens!" Foster exclaimed. "What did happen?"

He was told briefly. Speechless for a moment, he regarded Slade, finally saying, "The life you lead! I'd be a nervous wreck inside of a week, but you seem to thrive on it."

"I suppose one can get used to anything," El Halcon said carelessly. "By the way, keep what we told you under your sombrero. We'll let folks do a little guessing."

"I'll do that," Foster promised. "Well, I'll get back to my place. Feel a whole lot better."

"Thank you," Slade said soberly, for he appreciated Foster's concern.

The Branding Pen was buzzing over the mysterious shooting, so the truth of the matter was repeated for Mary's benefit, including Blaine Foster's reactions.

"I can sympathize with him," the girl said. "I know just how he felt. I'm on the verge of a nervous breakdown myself. I won't know a moment's peace until that awful man is either dead or in jail."

"One or the other soon," the sheriff comforted. "Don't bother your pretty head about it."

"I can't help doing so," Mary replied. "I doubt if any woman could."

"Have your dinner and you'll feel better," Crane

advised. "That always helps. And a snort or two. Waiter!"

He proceeded to follow his own advice.

"Wonder if Hale was with those wind spiders tonight?" he suddenly asked.

"I doubt it," Slade replied. "It was the kind of a chore he'd very likely give to his hired hands, not wishing to take the chance of being recognized. Also, there's just a chance that he was one of the tall pair I think I may have nicked in the course of the try made against Foster."

"Sure hope so," growled Crane. "Hope he picks up gangrene in a hurry."

"Not likely, in this clean, dry air," Slade said. "It is almost unknown in southwest Texas. Wounds, even serious ones, usually heal quickly, with no complications. That's the rule here."

"Well, here's hoping he proves to be the exception to the rule," Crane answered.

"You're presupposing that he was the one I nicked, if I really nicked either of them," Slade smiled. "But keep on hoping."

"And I'll help," Mary said.

"Bloodthirsty little tyke," Slade reproved laughingly.

"Where that awful man is concerned, I am," she replied, her big eyes flashing.

After a leisurely dinner and a glass of wine, Mary admitted she did feel better. She glanced around the room.

"Quieter and more peaceful than usual," she commented.

"We can stand a helpin' of both," said the sheriff. "I'd like a spell of not doing a thing, or thinking about anything. How about you, Walt?"

"Would do for a while, but I fear it would quickly become boresome," the Ranger replied. "When one is accustomed to living hard and fast, it's difficult to change."

"You wait till the years creep up on you," Crane retorted. "You'll see! You young hellions ain't happy unless you're mixed up in some kind of heck-raising, but just wait!"

"I'm younger than Walt, but I agree with you, Uncle Tom. What I'd like most is just a spell of doing nothing."

"Can I depend on that?" Slade asked, crinkling his eyes at her.

"Well, maybe," she replied demurely, lowering her lashes. The sheriff shook with laughter.

17

A few minutes later, Mary exclaimed animatedly, "I'd like to visit Mr. Foster's place again. Okay, Walt?"

"All right," he complied. "Wouldn't mind having a word with him myself."

"And I'll traipse along, just in case," said the sheriff.

Waving to Hardrock, they left the Branding Pen and soon reached the Big Enough, where they found Foster in a cheerful mood.

"Mr. Quimby leaves tomorrow morning," he said. "I plan to ride up to the spread tomorrow afternoon. Like to come along, Mr. Slade?"

"Wouldn't be a bad notion," El Halcon replied. "I'd like to give the holding a once-over."

Personally he thought it a very good notion, for he was not sure just what Griswold Hale's attitude toward Foster might be. Perhaps he had decided to pay the Big Enough owner no further mind, but then again he might still be motivated by a fear that Foster would eventually start talking about his past, and be anxious to eliminate him before he did.

The sheriff evidently experienced a similar feeling, for he nodded emphatic approval.

"Uncle John and Joyce and a couple more of

the boys will be in town around noon," Mary said. "I'll ride to the spread with them, but I'll be back the next day."

"I spoke to the coroner and he promised to hold the inquest on those dead outlaws shortly after noon," Foster said, "so we can get an early start."

With a busy day ahead, everybody called it an early night.

The inquest, which *was* held shortly after noon, was the usual cut and dried affair. The killing of Foster's assailants was justified. From the looks of the dead jigger picked up on Fourth Street, he was probably mixed up in some deviltry and got what was coming to him.

As a result, a little later Slade and Foster set out for the Four J spread.

As they rode, Foster chatted animatedly of his prospects, but Slade was mostly silent, constantly scanning the terrain over which they passed. When they entered the broken ground, his vigilance increased, although he hardly thought a drygulching would be staged there. Very likely Hale had other things to occupy his mind.

Just what those "other things" might be, Slade had not the slightest idea, but he experienced an uneasy presentiment that they boded no good for somebody.

However, they reached the Four J without untoward incident. There Slade met the hands and liked their looks. They were all pretty well along in years and were evidently glad to be able to sign on with the new owner. They might be a little slower than younger rannies, but competent and dependable. He felt Foster had made a wise choice.

After a cup and a snack prepared by the cook, who was also elderly, Slade and Foster set out to look the holding over. After a while the latter asked,

"Well, what do you think of it?"

"I think you got a bargain," was Slade's verdict. "Yes, I see no reason why you shouldn't do well. Good pasture. Those hills to the north are slashed by canyons and gulleys that will provide shelter for the cows in really bad weather, and you have much better water than Griswold Hale had before he drilled his wells."

"Hale's holding butts up against my land about two miles to the east of here," Foster remarked. "To the east of his spread, you know, is Fletcher Bartlett's Diamond F, with John Webb's Cross W to the south. I'll have good neighbors once we get rid of that horned toad, Hale. Guess that isn't the right thing to call him. What he really reminds me of is the Gila Monster we have over in Arizona—plumb pizen."

Slade laughed at the conceit and they rode on. And as they rode, he constantly studied the rugged hills to the north, which extended unbroken past Hale's spread and Bartlett's, who, like Hale, included their south section in his holding.

It was not only his concern for Foster's safety that motivated El Halcon when he accompanied the Four J owner to his holding. A plan had been building up in his mind that he felt might possibly bring results and which he resolved to put into action. As it had to do with the hills, the rugged range naturally interested him. Similar expedients had done so in the past.

The Four J cows were not numerous at present but they were excellent stock, which Slade commented on.

"And I'll soon have some more run in," Foster said. "Yep, I hope to have a real cow factory going before long."

A little later they circled back to the casa, arriving there at sunset. After a good dinner, they sat in the living room and smoked and talked.

"When do you plan to return to Sanderson?" Foster asked. "I think I'll stick around for a couple of days to get a better notion as to conditions and the lay of the land. My head bartender is reliable and will look after the Big Enough."

"A good idea," Slade said. "If you don't mind, I'll knock off a few hours of sleep and then slip out quietly and amble; I'd like to get an early start. I'll be careful not to disturb anybody."

"You go right ahead," Foster replied. "There'll

be a snack on the table, and with the fire banked in the stove, the coffee will keep warm. Go ahead as if the place was your own. Guess it is, in a way," he added with a grin, "seeing if it wasn't for you, I wouldn't be here to claim ownership. I'll leave a light on in the kitchen. Take the first room on the right at the head of the stairs."

In a good bed, Slade slept soundly until some three hours before daybreak. He arose and dressed and, moving in almost utter silence, as he could when he wished to, descended the stairs and consumed the coffee and the snack. After which he cinched up and rode away from the ranchhouse.

However, he did not continue toward Sanderson but turned north toward the dark loom of the hills.

He rode slowly, enjoying the star-strewn beauty of the night, for he was in no hurry. Thc roses of the dawn had not bloomed in the east when he reached the base of the hills. Close to the growth that clothed their slopes, he dismounted, flipped out the bit and loosened the cinches and turned Shadow loose to graze. Then he rolled a cigarette and stretched out comfortably to await the day.

Finally it came, in gold and scarlet splendor, the prairie sparkling with a myriad of dew gems that a little breeze shook down from the grassheads.

He waited a little longer before flipping back the bit and tightening the cinches and stood scanning the lonely rangeland in every direction.

"Horse," he said, "we're going to play another of our hunches. I feel pretty sure the outlaws have a hole-up somewhere in these up-ended hunks of rock. If we can find it, and I feel pretty sure we can, if there really is one, good may come of it. Not necessarily, but there's always a chance. Has happened more than once in the past. So get set to do a little scrambling and rooting."

Shadow snorted resignedly and tackled the slope.

Hour after hour, Slade rode through the hills, entering canyons, most of which were narrow and boxed. He studied gulleys and dry washes, searching for hoof prints and other evidence of the presence or passage of cattle or horses. The movements of birds on the wing and little animals in the brush received attention. And always he scanned the sky for that indubitable evidence of human occupancy—smoke.

But as the hours passed without results, he began to wonder if he were mistaken in his belief that the outlaws had a hangout in the rugged fastness. Began to look that way. However, he persevered, resolved not to give over the quest until darkness forced him to do so.

And then, well past noon, he struck pay dirt. It was a narrow canyon its entrance almost hidden by tall chaparral, that gave the appearance of being a box, with the open range no great distance from its mouth. He entered it, and his pulses quickened.

At the mouth the ground was soft and scored with the marks of cow hoofs and the prints of horses' irons. Some of which had been scored a short time before.

"Shadow," he said, "I believe this is it. Sure looks a lot that way. Stretch your long ears, now, and keep your eyes open. No telling what may be around the next bend, and this crack appears to have plenty. Scoured out by water that followed the path of least resistance, ages and ages ago."

With every sense at hair-trigger alertness, he rode slowly up the canyon, which wound about like a snake with the itch. Abruptly he drew rein and sat listening. Faint with distance had sounded what was without doubt the grumbling bawl of a peevish steer. At the same moment, he sniffed sharply.

"Been a fire kindled in here, not recently, but not so long ago, either," he muttered. "This is getting plumb interesting."

He slowed Shadow to a walk and rode on, peering and listening. Again came the grumble of cattle, but no other sound broke the stillness, save the chirping of birds in the thickets. They did not sound disturbed, which was reassuring.

Another quarter of a mile or so and again he halted, staring.

As he expected it would be, the canyon was a box, a sheer cliff rising to a dizzy height only a couple of hundred yards ahead.

But what held Slade's attention was a rough corral built so that the end wall and the side wall of the gorge provided two sides of the enclosure. And behind those corral bars were more than fifty head of prime beef critters. A single glance at their brands told Slade they were Fletcher Bartlett's Diamond F stock. So Hale and his devils had been busy.

A familiar story in this section. Run off the critters in the night time, foil pursuit, hole them up in the hills during daylight, then, under cover of darkness, run them south to the Rio Grande, the fords, and the waiting buyers. He had discovered Hale's cow hole-up.

Just one flaw in the picture. Nowhere could he see any signs of a hole-up for men. No old cabin or shack built by trappers or hunters of bygone days. Nor could he see any evidence of a fire having been lighted, although his sensitive nostrils still caught the scent of a burning not so long before.

"Anyhow," he breathed to Shadow, "there sure doesn't appear to be anybody around. So let's do a mite of investigating."

Shooting glances in every direction, the knotted reins dropped on the horse's neck, both hands close to his guns, he rode ahead. He had nearly reached the box wall when suddenly the mystery was resolved.

Almost hidden by an overlap of stone was a dark opening in the face of the cliff, undoubtedly the mouth of a cave. Once again he halted his mount and sat gazing at the opening. No sound came from it. There was no sign of movement. He decided to take a chance.

Dismounting, he glided forward on foot, reached the opening and stood flattened against the cliff wall beside it, straining his ears.

Reassured by the continual silence, he peered in. But the gloom inside was dense and he could make out nothing. He fumbled three matches from his pocket, grouped them together and struck them.

The quick flare of flame showed that this was without a doubt the hidden hangout. There were bunks built against thc walls of thc cavc, stacks of feed, and staple provisions. Cooking utensils beside what appeared to be a stone fireplace, a home-made table and several home-made chairs. Comfortable enough for a temporary occupancy.

The cave was not large, a mere grotto of some ten feet in width by perhaps twice that in length.

Well, he had found it, but what the devil was he to do with it? Hole up and wait for the outlaws to put in an appearance, hoping to get the drop on them? Very good, were his opinion that Hale had but two followers left the correct one. But there was no guarantee of the correctness of that opinion. Others of his former associates might have drifted east and joined up with him. It would be gambling his life against a surmise. Far from a sensible thing to do. He dropped the match sticks and stepped out of the cave to consider the matter. His gaze focused on the cattle in the corral.

Suddenly he chuckled; a thought had struck him. Would be a rather foolhardy thing to do, but darned if he didn't believe he'd risk it. Would be turning the tables on the wideloopers with a vengeance. Still chuckling, he strode to Shadow and mounted.

"Okay, horse, here's where we go back into the cow business," he said. He rode to the entrance of the corral, which was spanned by a crude gate with leather hinges. Reaching down, he unlatched the gate and swung it open.

The cattle at once streamed out. Slade herded them down the canyon.

The first part of the chore was simple enough; the critters could not stray. However, it was a ticklish business, not knowing from one minute to the next what he might meet around one of the bends. He felt fairly confident the outlaws would not head for the canyon to move the purloined stock before dark, and there were still several hours of daylight, but even of that he was not sure. He breathed relief when he reached the open prairie, where he would have at least a fighting chance were he intercepted. A sweeping glance showed nobody in sight.

Getting so large a herd in marching order and headed in the right direction was something of a chore for one man, but El Halcon, a tophand, finally accomplished it. The cows rolled on toward their home pasture, Fletcher Bartlett's range.

Slade chuckled more than once as he shoved the herd along, for he felt he had very neatly put one over on Hale and his devils. He would have given much to see the outlaw leader's expression and hear what he had to say when he discovered the herd missing. He'd very likely really be fit to be hogtied.

Progress was slow with the heavily-fleshed beefs. The sun dropped down the slant of the western sky. Slade rode along the marching column, veering the leaders more to the south. Now, he knew, he was on Bartlett's holding, but still quite a few miles from his casa. But with no bad luck he would make it before sundown. And so far, everything was going smoothly.

18

Then abruptly the "smoothness" roughened up a bit. Shadow began blowing softly through his nose. Slade glanced to the right, to the left, over his shoulder. His gaze centered.

Far to the rear, a thousand yards, maybe a little more, four horsemen were riding in his direction. They rode swiftly, and purposefully. Slade studied them. Could be just some of Bartlett's hands hunting for their lost cows. He continued to study the group.

Another moment and his keen eyes noted something which banished that hope. The faces of the riders were not whitish blurs but dark smudges; they were masked. Hale and his sidewinders without a doubt. And evidently he had managed to enlist another follower.

"And looks like I miscalculated a bit," Slade remarked to his horse. "They didn't wait until after dark to head for the canyon. Well, let them get a little closer and we'll see." He fingered the butt of his Winchester, glanced anxiously westward. Just the upper rim of the sun was showing and shadows were beginning to curdle under the clumps of growth scattered over the prairie. Which wasn't so good. Darkness would not help his cause. He gazed back at the pursuing horsemen, and abruptly the situation took a turn for the worse.

Two of the riders separated from the group. One rode south by slightly east, the other north by slightly east.

Slade at once understood the meaning of the maneuver. Their intention was to surround him and attack from three sides. And because of the comparatively slow pace of the cattle, they'd succeed in doing just that. Of course he could abandon the herd and Shadow would quickly show a clean set of heels to any pursuit. But he was hanged if he was going to; at least, only as a last resort. Not after all the work and trouble he had undergone in recovering it. He glanced ahead and saw something else that boded no good.

No great distance to the front was a narrow but long straggle of chaparral extending from north to south. He'd have to bypass that line of growth, which would give the encircling outlaws plenty of time to complete their movement and hole up in the brush where, with the light swiftly fading, the advantage would be theirs.

Now the pair behind, one of which Slade felt sure was Griswold Hale, were closing the distance a bit, but still out of rifle range. They'd speed up only after their two companions had achieved their encircling objective and were set for business. Slade turned his eyes to the front. The belt of thicket was now not far away. And the pair aiming to surround him had vanished from sight. He resolved on a last daring expedient that might work. Riding swiftly to the head of the column, he veered the leaders more to the east, their noses pointing straight for the bristle of chaparral.

Whirling Shadow, he rode back to drag the rear of the cows, flipped loose his sixty-foot throwing rope and belabored the rumps of the rearmost cows, whooping and yelling.

The drag cows bawled with pain and fright and surged forward, slamming into those in front of them. Slade continued to roar and wield the rope.

Now the panic was spreading to the lead cattle. Another moment and a full-fledged stampede was under way, the bellowing cows streaking forward, straight for the wall of not too thick brush. Now nothing less than a stone wall would stop them until they got over their terror or distanced that mad thing howling and slashing behind them.

The terrified herd hit the growth like a cyclone on the loose, went tearing through it. Shadow, doubtless cursing the day he was born, stormed after the fleeing beefs. A few minutes of wild conquest of the growth and the lead critters burst through the eastern fringe and went pounding east by slightly south, toward their home pasture, the rest of the herd streaming after them.

Slade cleared the chaparral. Racing down from the north and only a few hundred yards distant was a man mounted on a foaming horse. Slade flung the Winchester to the front; two reports boomed as one.

A slug tore through the leg of Slade's overalls, but the riding outlaw spun from his saddle to the ground. A second bullet flicked El Halcon's hat sideways and he whirled to face the second outlaw surging up from the south. The light was fading, the tall brush casting shadows, back and forth through which stabbed lances of fire. The outlaw's mount was rearing and plunging, Shadow doing a shifting dance, his rider weaving and ducking.

Slade's voice rang out,

"Steady!"

Instantly the tall black horse halted to stand motionless. The owlhoot, caught off balance by the unexpectedness of the move, tried to line sights, but before he could squeeze trigger, he fell, his breast riddled by the Winchester slugs.

Without a glance at the two still forms, Slade sent Shadow flying east. His one great desire was to put distance between himself and the belt of chaparral before the following pair reached it and opened fire on him from cover. Twisting in the saddle, he sprayed the growth with lead until the magazine was empty; might hold them up a bit. He reloaded with frantic speed and fired a couple more shots.

There were no answering reports, and now

he was a full six hundred yards away from the froth and practically out of danger; and still the thicket remained silent, and dusk was gathering. Evidently Hale and the devil with him had decided to give up and were headed elsewhere.

"Well, we came out of it very well," he told Shadow. "Just a few welts and scratches; not bad. How you feel?"

Shadow did not deign to reply vocally—his thorn-scraped hide was answer enough. Slade chuckled and gazed back at the gloomy stand of chaparral.

"Thought at first you were all set to hand me my quietus," he remarked to the thorny tangle. "But you ended up doing me a real good turn. Thanks!"

He rode on after the cows, which, having run themselves into a state of near-exhaustion, were plodding along doggedly, east by south. Now, the Ranger knew, the Diamond F casa was little more than a mile or so distant. He rode on, feeling quite well pleased with himself. Hale had escaped, per usual, but had undoubtedly been dealt a staggering jolt. And unless he managed to tie onto some more, the outlaw number was reduced to a couple. All in all, not a bad day's work.

A little later, he sighted the casa by the fading light, and still a little later he could make out figures moving about the ranchhouse yard.

Quite likely the Diamond F hands had heard the shooting and were wondering what it was about.

The activity increased as the weary cattle jogged nearer, and men started running forward, Fletcher Bartlett, the owner, in the lead. A few more minutes and they were close.

"What the blinkin' blue blazes!" bawled Bartlett. "Slade! Where the devil did you get those cows?"

"You shouldn't allow them to stray about in the hills," the Ranger replied reprovingly. "They're not safe up there."

"In the hills the devil!" howled Bartlett. "They were widelooped last night and run to the Rio Grande."

"Made a fast trip back," Slade said.

"Please!" the Diamond F owner pleaded. "Please tell me what's the meaning of this. Do you want me to have a stroke?"

"I think you're immune," Slade answered, and detailed briefly the day's episode. Bartlett swore and shook his head.

"You're the limit!" he declared. "Anybody else would have been done for a half dozen times over. And you did for two of the wind spiders? Fine! What about their bodies?"

"Leave them," Slade directed. "I want the sheriff to see them as they are. But you might send somebody to round up the horses and bring them in. I didn't think it would be wise for me to stop and look after them. Good critters. Put them in your corral."

"Sure for certain," Bartlett replied, and dispatched a couple of hands to care for the chore.

"And now," Slade said as he dismounted, "I could stand a bite to eat and a surrounding for my horse. I'll give him a couple of hours rest and then I'm heading for Sanderson."

"Everything coming up," Bartlett assured him. "Come on in and take a load off your feet. Here's a jigger who used to take care of Shadow; he'll look after him. Come on in."

After eating, Slade examined the two horses that had been brought in. The brand on one proved to be an Arizona burn he recognized; it had not been altered.

Meant nothing aside from confirming his opinion that Hale's former associates were still drifting east and signing up with him. Were he able to continue to run around loose, he might well get another bunch together. And, Slade was forced to grudgingly admit, he still had nothing on the slippery devil that would stand up in court. Well, maybe he'd ultimately blunder; his kind almost always did, sooner or later.

Shadow had had a rather rough day, and Slade allowed him another hour of rest before cinching up and heading for Sanderson, Bartlett still expressing his gratitude for the return of his cows, which represented quite a sum of money.

Slade did not push his mount, and it was past midnight when he reached town and cared for the tired animal. Then he moseyed to the Branding Pen, where, as he very well knew he would, he found Mary and the sheriff awaiting him.

"Another little wagon chore for you," he told Crane.

"How many this time?" the sheriff asked. "What! Only two? You're slippin'. How'd you come to tie onto them?"

Slade told them briefly, while they listened with absorbed interest.

"So they did have a hangout in the hills, eh?" Crane remarked.

"Yes; almost universally the case with an outfit like that. A place where they can lie low for a while, if it is expedient to do so, and to get together to plan their raids."

"Think they'll be going back there?"

"Unlikely, I'd say," Slade replied. "Doubtful if they'd take the chance, although there's no telling what Hale might do. Not apt to be any more widelooping, unless he manages to enlist a few more followers; that's not a chore for two men, no matter how competent."

"You figure he'll strike someplace else?" asked Crane.

"Undoubtedly," Slade answered. "Unless my analysis of him is completely wrong, he is a person who can't stand frustration of any kind.

A non-conformist, a rebel against society—a case of stark individualism run riot, battening on cruelty and slaughter, by way of which he achieves a feeling of superiority over his fellow men. Yes, he'll strike again, and soon, I feel safe in predicting. And very likely whatever depredation he has in mind will be accompanied by murder. That's *amigo* Griswold Hale. And it's up to us to do our best to stop him before some other innocent person dies."

"As Blaine Foster would have were it not for you," said Crane. "Well, my money's still on El Halcon. How about you, Mary?"

"To the last peso," the girl replied. "Suppose we call it a night."

19

Shortly before noon, the "carcass cart," as Deputy Bert Ester dubbed the wagon, rolled east by north, pausing briefly at Fletcher Bartlett's casa, continuing to the scene of the gunfight near the thicket.

The bodies were right where Slade had left them.

"Not even a coyote or a buzzard would touch 'em," growled the sheriff. "They don't hanker to be pizened. Let's see what's in their pockets."

The pockets produced nothing other than money, which Crane transferred to his own. Nobody recalled seeing the pair before.

"You'll notice they are both men along in years," Slade remarked to Crane. "Yes, undoubtedly some of the old Arizona bunch with which Hale was associated. Well, here's hoping there will be no more mavericking this way. Okay, let's load 'em up."

Sanderson was reached without incident. An inquest, of sorts, was held, and the bodies consigned to Boot Hill.

Several peaceful days followed. So peaceful, in fact, that the sheriff grew distinctly nervous. Slade remained composed, for there was nothing to do but wait, and fussing about it wouldn't help. Mary was very well satisfied with things as they were.

"Nice, not having to hold my breath until you show up," she said to Slade.

Then, the evening of the third day, Griswold Hale, his usual assured self, entered the Branding Pen where Slade was eating his dinner with Mary and the sheriff. He nodded cordially.

Slade returned the nod. Mary waved her hand. Sheriff Crane also managed a nod, although Slade feared he would succumb to apoplexy as a result.

"Watch your expression," he warned. "I think he has his eye on our reflection in the back bar mirror."

Hale didn't approach the table, nor did he stay long. A couple of drinks and he sauntered out, waving goodnight.

The sheriff did so, with an effort, and continued to put away his surrounding as if nothing had happened.

"Now what!" snorted the sheriff. "Wonder why he's in town tonight? Think he aims to pull something?"

"It is possible," Slade replied. "However, I somehow don't think so. I'd say he's just looking things over, in search, perhaps, of what appears a likely prospect two men could handle. Surmise on my part, but I believe I'm right. If he does have something in mind and pulls it, we'll hear about it soon enough."

"The impudence of the hellion!" growled Crane. "Walkin' in here big as life and twice as ornery!"

"He knows we have nothing on him," Slade pointed out. "May actually not give us credit for suspecting him, although I think he's just a mite too smart for that.

"I've been nosing about a bit and learned a few things," Slade added. "Had a talk with Childress of the bank, who knows I'm a Ranger. He told me Hale made only a down payment, not very large, when he bought the Rocking L, and that he negotiated a small loan at the bank, with the cows on the spread as security—there are not many of them—to purchase the drilling outfit."

"Which means," guessed the sheriff, "that if he managed to make one more good haul, he might pull out of the section?"

"Not beyond the realm of possibility," Slade replied. "I hope not; I've no desire to chase him all over Texas, or elsewhere. Well, we'll see."

But if Hale did have something in mind, he did not translate it into action. The night passed without any overt act on the part of Hale or anybody else.

The following morning was also peaceful, so far, although it was a yellow morning, hot and sultry and very still.

And then the weather gods, a cantankerous and unpredictable lot, decided to take a hand and give the section a little taste of what *they* could do if they were of a mind to.

Out of the south there drifted a monstrous cloud, purple and piled, climbing slowly up the hushed heaven, forked lightning flashing from its breast. It obscured the sun and an eerie twilight shrouded the landscape. Leaves drooped in the trees. Birds ceased their calling and cowered in the thickets. The cattle were still save for uneasy moanings as they huddled together. It seemed that nothing moved save only the great cloud which rolled up and onward, with fold on fold from the black horizon, until the whole vast sweep of the southern sky was one great leaden arch.

It crossed over Sanderson, to the accompaniment of thunder mutterings and the vivid gleam of lightning. Then that cloud proceeded to exemplify Louis the Fourteenth's famous remark, "After me the deluge!"

It was a deluge, all right; a veritable cloudburst. That cloud seemingly burst wide open and dumped its contents on the Sanderson area in one fell swoop.

Water cascaded from the cliff tops, roared down the canyon, leaving death and destruction in its wake. Such sturdy edifices as the Regan House, the courthouse, the railroad station, and those that housed the Branding Pen, the Big Enough and other business establishments, withstood the fury of the flood. Shadow's stable, entrenched between two firm buildings, suffered only minor damage.

But it was different with the poorly constructed cabins, shacks, and flimsy false fronts. They were destroyed or swept away.

Lightning flashed in one continuous sheet of flame. Thunder rolled deafeningly, an uninterrupted blast of horrific sound. Raindrops driven on the wings of the shrieking wind shattered glass and stung the flesh like shot. The cries of the injured were drowned by the incessant cannonading of the warring elements. Tragedy indeed stalked naked through the land.

The terrible day wore on. The rain still fell, but not nearly so violently. The cataracts from the cliffs and the upper canyon quickly lessened. The eerie twilight merged to blackest night, through which gleamed lanterns and flares and torches as those in a condition to do so strode forth to minister to the stricken.

Sheriff Crane swore in special deputies who patrolled the stricken town. There were some sporadic attempts at looting by the irresponsible, but a little well-placed lead quickly discouraged that.

Walt Slade was everywhere, Mary Merril trudging beside him despite his protests. He led numb and bewildered people to safety, treated injuries as best he could, probed the wreckage for possible survivors. They discovered one man pinned by debris, the water slowly rising about him, almost reaching his straining chin. With his great strength, Slade managed to tear away the timbers that held him prisoner and hauled him out, bruised and battered and cut, but not seriously, and able to express his profound gratitude.

The rain ceased. The ominous cloud rolled away and the stars blossomed. And finally the east flushed rose and scarlet and gold and came the day, the sun shining brightly in a sky of purest blue to outline the scene of disaster in all its hideous details.

The railroad yards were a shambles. East and west the main line tracks had been washed away. Sanderson was isolated so far as rail traffic was concerned.

But with the true pioneer spirit, the survivors of the holocaust began at once the task of restoring.

Help poured in from the neighboring ranches, manpower, food, clothing, blankets.

"The Galveston flood in miniature," Slade remarked to Mary as he straightened his aching back.

"You saw that, didn't you, dear?" she asked.

"Yes, I was there," he replied. "It was far worse than this. The hurricane-driven water from the Gulf rose four feet in as many seconds and washed clear across the island. Thousands died and the town was almost totally destroyed.

"But Galveston came back," he added. "Just as Sanderson will come back. You can't keep the American spirit down. Now you'd better toddle to bed before you topple over. I will, too, after I have a talk with Crane."

"Okay," she agreed. "I'll admit I can hardly keep my eyes open. Did I do all right?"

"You did wonderfully," he assured her. "You are of the breed that won the West."

Yes, Sanderson would come back, despite, literally, hell and high water. It proceeded to do so. The railroad would quickly be put back in running shape, the yards cleaned up. Damage was being repaired, new buildings already planned.

Slade slept soundly for several hours and awakened to discover he was ravenous. He arose and dressed quietly, so as to not disturb anybody, and headed for the Branding Pen, pausing at Shadow's stable to make sure he was all right, which he was.

When he entered the Branding Pen, he found Sheriff Crane there.

"Thought you'd be happening along about now," the sheriff said.

"You haven't been to bed?"

"Oh, I knocked off a little snooze in my chair," the rugged old peace officer replied. "That'll hold me until tonight. Little gal sure stuck by you through all that hell."

“Yes, she sure did,” Slade said. “She’s a wonder.”

“Well, if that sidewinder Hale had any notions, the storm sure knocked ’em galleywest,” Crane remarked. “Some little good came out of it.”

“But he’ll make up for lost time, on that you can rely,” Slade said.

“Maybe he got washed away,” the sheriff observed hopefully.

“I fear he’s not the washing-away kind,” Slade smiled. “But the flood sure didn’t play any favorites; raised the devil with everything that wasn’t firmly foundationed.

“The last big rain, I predicted that something like this would happen someday,” he added reflectively. “But I sure didn’t think it would come so soon, although it was to be expected from any really bad storm. The canyon is a natural drainage for all the surrounding water on all sides.”

“And she sure came down on all sides,” said Crane. “Reminded me of what I’ve heard Niagara Falls looks like. Well, here’s the chuck and I feel like putting away a hefty helpin’. How about you?”

“I’ll admit I’m about ready to topple over,” Slade replied. “Haven’t had a bite, not even a swig of coffee, for about twenty-four hours; rather busy hours at that.”

With which conversation ceased for quite some time.

Finally the sheriff pushed back his empty plate with a satisfied sigh and ordered a snort.

While he was enjoying it, Hardrock came over to join them for a few minutes.

"Yep, we got off easy," he said. "A couple of inches of water on the floor, but that was all. This shack is set up sorta high on the foundation, and the ground here, like over on Railroad Street, is a mite higher than most."

"Which reminds me," Slade said. "I want to drop in at the Big Enough and learn how Foster made out."

"Heard his place wasn't damaged much, either," Hardrock replied. "As I said, Railroad Street is on a bit of a rise. But the yards, which are lower, sure caught it. Won't take those jiggers long to put things back in shape, though."

"Same goes for the railroad," remarked Crane. "They'll be runnin' trains in another day or two. Oh, I guess it could have been worse. Bad enough, though; several poor devils got drowned, and a couple of kids, I heard. Strange how young folks gets knocked off and old sticks like myself are left standing. Must be somehow for the best though, I reckon; we never know what the future may turn up."

Slade did visit the Big Enough, a little later, and found that, like the Branding Pen, aside from a wet floor it had not suffered much.

"But it looked bad for a time," Foster said. "The

water kept rising and rising, and you could hear the beams creaking and the shingles grinding together. Was afraid the foundations would be washed out. We came through all right, though, which is more than you can say for some other places.

"Hasn't hurt business, either," he said, gesturing to the crowded bar.

When Slade returned to the Branding Pen, he found Mary there.

"So, got your beauty sleep, eh?" he remarked. "You look it."

"I didn't look it this morning, though. Hair stringy, covered with mud, shirt and overalls shrinking."

"Shrinking didn't do any harm," said the sheriff. "Fact is it sorta improved things, from my way of—looking."

"You would!" she retorted. "That's the man of it. But I don't believe Walt even noticed."

"Why should he?" the sheriff asked pointedly.

Mary did not deign to reply.

20

Sanderson continued to dig out. The damage to the railroad was repaired, trains began running on schedule again. The yards were already in pretty good shape. All was bustle and activity, and optimism. The dead were buried, and soon forgotten. Death sharp and sudden was too common an occurrence in the frontier country to make any lasting impression, except on those directly concerned.

Soon the town would be going about its business as usual.

Twice, Griswold Hale appeared in town, but so did all the other owners of the neighborhood. Anyhow, nothing resulted from his visits, so far as Slade was able to ascertain. However, it did look a little like he was keeping an eye on something. What, Slade hadn't the slightest idea.

Having designated Sanderson a disaster area, the State also proceeded to lend assistance. An old express car, apparently very much in need of repairs, was detached from the late evening local and shunted onto a spur track in the yards, where it was left.

A little later, Childress, the banker, who was still in his office although it was long past the bank's closing time, sent for Slade.

“Walt,” he said, when the Ranger arrived, “there is something I think you should know. It’s supposed to be a dead secret, but my experience with ‘dead secrets’ is that all too often they are anything but secret, especially when cooked up by folks over at the Capital who are not familiar with conditions in these outlying sections.”

He paused to light a cigar. Slade rolled a cigarette. When the smokes were going in a satisfactory manner, he continued,

“It has to do with that old express car that came in with the local and was shoved into the yards. In that car is a safe, and in the safe is a large sum of money, a state grant for repairs and new buildings. The money is to be transferred to the bank in the morning, under guard. But at present there are no guards in or around the car. Elaborate precautions, so called, have been taken to cause that car to appear just what it is supposed to be, an old piece of equipment in need of repairs. That’s the scheme the boys over at the State House have evolved, who I think have been a bit jittery since the train robbery.

“Fine—if nobody but myself and the General Yardmaster knows the truth! Yes, quite a scheme, if it works, and nobody else catches on. What do you think?”

“In my opinion,” Slade replied quietly, “that car merits a little attention. Yes, a very neat scheme; appearing, on the surface, fool proof.

But unfortunately such things seldom are; too many people involved, and the scheme wholly dependent on the premise that nobody will guess or learn the truth about that car. And at present there are individuals in the section who appear able to learn anything they desire to learn.

"I'm glad you told me this, Ron," he concluded. "May help to solve a problem of my own."

"Anyhow," said the banker, with a smile, "I feel much less anxious about the safety of that money the town so badly needs."

Slade left the banker's office in a pleased, even jubilant mood, for he experienced a premonition that here at last was showdown. Yes, before the night was over, he believed, it would be the last roundup for either Griswold Hale or himself. Well, he welcomed the chance and if Hale did contemplate a raid on the money car and was accompanied by but one follower, he was fairly sanguine as to the outcome. If he happened to have enlisted more—that would quite likely be a different story. All in the day's work! And if your number isn't up, nobody can put it up! He turned his steps to the Branding Pen with a tranquil mind.

The sheriff, pretty well worn out, had gone to bed early, saying he would be up by midnight. Mary had also sought a little more rest. So Slade sat alone, smoking and sipping coffee, reviewing his plan of action. Being familiar with the yards, he knew where the spur on which the express car sat was located. It was at the far end of the yards, well away from the centers of activity. By midnight that portion of the yards would be nearly if not wholly deserted, more likely the latter.

He did not think the outlaws would strike before or a little after midnight and laid his plans accordingly. A bit past eleven o'clock he left the Branding Pen and reached the yards by a circuitous route. At a spot in the shadow between a couple of tall hoppers, from where he had a clear view of the express car, he took up his post to watch and wait. Now all this section of the yards was silent, and dark save for the glow of the switch lights. But one taller light, that marked a lead, dimly outlined the car.

From a cunningly concealed pocket in his broad leather belt, Slade produced the famous silver star set on a silver circle, the honored badge of the Texas Rangers, and pinned it to his shirt front. The authority it represented might possibly cause one of the outlaws to surrender, although he did not think Griswold Hale would be that one. Wishing for the cigarette he dared not light, he lounged against the steel side of the hopper and waited.

The wait proved longer than he expected, until he began to wonder uneasily if he had guessed wrong; if Hale had not learned about the money car and therefore did not plan to make a try for it. Could be; the whole business was based on surmise.

And then at the rear end of the car he sensed movement, which materialized into two figures that stole up the steps to the rear platform; paused. To Slade's sensitive ear came the tiny click of a turned key. The pair disappeared inside the car, closing the door behind them. Another moment and a soft glow birthed behind the car window.

Slade waited a few more minutes; must get the devils dead to rights. In the Fenwick Store robbery, the safe's combination knob had been drilled out. Doubtless the same procedure would be followed here.

Another moment and he glided to the steps, mounted them and with the greatest caution gripped the door knob, turning it by almost imperceptible degrees until the bolt was all the way back. Flinging the door wide open, he stepped inside, drawing both guns.

On the floor was a bull's eye lantern, its beam directed on the door of the safe. And in front of the safe squatted a man manipulating a hand drill. Another man, tall, broad-shouldered, masked, stood beside him. They whirled as Slade's voice thundered through the car,

"Up, you're covered! Trail's end, Hale, you are under arrest for robbery and murder, anything you say—"

Griswold Hale's reaction was an animal howl of rage and a hand darting to the gun at his belt.

Slade fired point-blank. Hale reeled back and back. The other man, given an instant's respite, jerked his gun and shot at the weaving, ducking Ranger. Slade's Colts boomed answer. The car rocked and quivered to the bellow of the reports.

Seconds later Walt Slade, blood dripping from his left hand and trickling down his cheek, lowered his smoking guns and peered through the powder fog at the two forms sprawled on the floor. He strode forward, holstering his guns, and ripped the mask from Hale's face. The outlaw leader glared up at him with glazing eyes of hellish hate. His gaze centered on the gleaming silver star.

"A—a Ranger!" he gasped. "They told me—I—couldn't—buck—the—Rangers!"

With his eyes fixed on the symbol of law and order and justice for all, he died.

The other outlaw was already dead. Slade spared him but a glance. Straightening up wearily, he gazed down at the dead face of the brilliant man who had taken the wrong fork of the trail.

Removing the star, he restored it to its pocket and stepped out of the car. Shouts were sounding, drawing nearer. Yardmen, attracted by the shouting, were approaching. One recognized him and called his name.

"Somebody fetch the sheriff," Slade ordered.

"I think you'll find him at the Branding Pen."

Two men darted off to attend to the chore. Slade leaned against the side of the car and rolled a cigarette, replying briefly to the questions volleyed at him.

"Yes, there's money in the safe," he said. "Two owlhoots tried to tie onto it. Go ahead and take a look at them, if you wish."

The railroaders did so, and came out buzzing. "Griswold Hale!" one exclaimed. "Wouldn't have believed it!"

Which was the general reaction later when the word got around.

The sheriff arrived; with him, Mary Merril.

"Oh, darling, you're hurt!" she exclaimed to Slade. "You're bleeding!"

"Just a couple of scratches," he replied. "You may patch them up when we reach the Branding Pen, if it'll make you feel better."

"Did you get him?" Crane asked.

"What's left of him and the other one, is in there," Slade answered. "Yes, showdown, and trail's end."

Now several bewildered railroad policemen were on hand, questioning, exclaiming.

"Keep a watch on this car and what's in it the rest of the night," the sheriff told them. "That is, except those two carcasses. Some of you work dodgers pack *them* to my office; Deputy Ester is there."

At the Branding Pen, Mary quickly cared for the two slight bullet cuts Slade had suffered. Then all three sat down to drinks and coffee, served by Hardrock Hogan in person.

"You riding right away?" the sheriff asked.

"I am not," Slade declared flatly. "I'm taking my vacation, what's left of it, right here. Then I'll mosey back to the Post to see what Captain Jim has lined up for me next."

"And after that," Mary said softly, her eyes somber, "the trail!"

Center Point Large Print
600 Brooks Road / PO Box 1
Thorndike, ME 04986-0001 USA

(207) 568-3717

US & Canada:
1 800 929-9108
www.centerpointlargeprint.com